668: THE NEIGHBOR OF THE BEAST

LIONEL FENN

ACE BOOKS, NEW YORK

This book is an Ace original edition, and has never been previously published.

668: THE NEIGHBOR OF THE BEAST

An Ace Book / published by arrangement with the author

PRINTING HISTORY
Ace edition / October 1992

ISBN: 0-441-76837-7

Ace Books are published by The Berkley Publishing Group,
200 Madison Avenue, New York, New York 10016.
The name "ACE" and the "A" logo are trademarks belonging to Charter Communications, Inc.

PRINTED IN THE UNITED STATES OF AMERICA

10 9 8 7 6 5 4 3 2 1

Z 50

PRAISE FOR THE KENT MONTANA BOOKS:

"Fenn cheerfully demolishes every cliché of every science fiction monster movie you've ever seen."

—Craig Shaw Gardner, bestselling author of *The Cineverse Cycle*

"Provides chuckles and non-stop action. Good fun!"

—*On Books*

"Fans of Craig Shaw Gardner will enjoy these books."

—*Raymond's Reviews*

"Lightweight and funny farce." —*Kliatt*

"Fenn lampoons the entire theme on a scale unrivaled since *The Girl, The Gold Watch, and Everything.*"

—*S. F. Chronicle*

DON'T MISS A SINGLE KENT MONTANA ADVENTURE!

Kent Montana and the Really Ugly Thing from Mars
IT is big. IT is ugly. IT has a heat ray and a nasty disposition. IT is, in short, the worst thing to happen to New Jersey since the last election.

Kent Montana and the Reasonably Invisible Man
A mad scientist has discovered the secret of (temporary) invisibility. He's not planning to sneak into the movies, either. He's mad, remember? He wants revenge!

Kent Montana and the Once and Future Thing
Down on the bayou, a man-eating she-beast is looking for a little affection. Or possibly . . . commitment. And guess who the swamp-mistress has fallen for?

The Mark of the Moderately Vicious Vampire
He turns into a bat. Drinks the blood of the living. And never pays income taxes. He's the Vampire Lamar, and he seeks a female companion to share his eternal night-life . . . in a *very* long-term relationship.

Ace Books by Lionel Fenn

KENT MONTANA AND THE REALLY UGLY THING FROM MARS
KENT MONTANA AND THE REASONABLY INVISIBLE MAN
KENT MONTANA AND THE ONCE AND FUTURE THING
THE MARK OF THE MODERATELY VICIOUS VAMPIRE
668: THE NEIGHBOR OF THE BEAST

The far reaches of Outer Space, as it is known to the many dedicated men and women who study those far reaches, and Outer Space, are filled with a lot of space that has been around, and empty, for millions of years;

The far reaches of Outer Space, besides having all that empty space, are also filled with celestial bodies, not a single one of which has been proven conclusively to contain any sort of Intelligent Life as we know it here on Earth;

On the other hand, Old Deities, Ronald Reagan, and Elvis have to come from somewhere and it certainly isn't New Jersey, so why not Outer Space is the question we feel this film explores in an intelligent and probing manner, along with a searing exposé of Soap Operas, just in case.

—Lionel Fenn
(your humble director)

668: THE NEIGHBOR OF THE BEAST

– I –

Director's Cut

✦1✦

The city, pondered Kent Montana.

Ah, the city!

The teeming millions, the hustle, the bustle, the excitement, the sensual danger of Wall Street's financial machinations, the dazzling nightlife of the sophisticated cabaret scene, the glitter of the seductive Broadway stage, the glow that permeates the magical silver screen, the filth, the crud, the absolutely disgusting—

✦2✦

Cut!

What! What did I say?

Kent, you're supposed to be extolling the virtues of New York, not the reality. Besides, you're ad-libbing.

I never.

I ought to know what I wrote.

I thought it might add a little verisimilitude to the opening scene.

Bullshit.

That, too.

Take it again.

✦1, again✦

The city, mused Kent Montana as he stood in front of his luxury townhouse, newly acquired through the last will and testament of a dear departed friend, is the Fabled Fount of Youth, the Marvelous Mecca of Wealth, the Astounding Arbiter of Culture, the Distinctive Designer of Taste, the Loquacious Leader of World Politics and Foreign Policy even though the Mayor isn't the President but probably thinks he ought to be.

It is, he contemplated further as he examined the tree-studded length and expensive automobile breadth of Langford Place, strangled by greedy unions, smothered by politicians who don't know their asses from a ballot box, being destroyed from within by the cankerous malaise that besets the entire human race at a time when—

✦3✦

Cut!

Again?

Kent. Kent. What is this, our fifth feature film together, right?

If you can call it that, yes, I suppose it is.

And have I ever steered you wrong during all that time?

Lionel, you blew up my apartment in Gander Pond.

Well . . .

You made me go to Louisiana in the middle of the summer and hang around with a guy named Joe Bill.

Well . . .

I had to listen to Zero Zuller, the sometimes blind musician with the cashmere golf cap, play "God Save the Queen" fifteen times on the bleedin' accordion.

Cruel, Kent, cruel.

You can say that again.

Look. Once this film is over, you'll have your own production company, right? That means you can do anything you want. Why, you don't even have to have me as your director anymore; all you have to do is say the word and I'm out of your life forever.

The word.

Not funny, Kent.

I'm in New York, Lionel. I don't feel funny.

Try it again.

The word.

Not that! The other thing.

Oh. Damn.

✦1, yet again✦

The city, ruminated Kent Montana.

Ah, the city!

What can I say that would adequately capture in words, in deed, in thought, in action, the eclectic electricity that flows through its veins, the magma-like magnetism that attracts the world's immaculate intellectuals and artistic geniuses to its generous bosom, the salaciously sweet siren song that lures young and old alike to its plenitude of promises of untold riches and everlasting fame.

By what humble communicative means at my humble disposal may I describe to those who have never been here the goddamn noise, the goddamn litter, the goddamn—

✦4✦

Cut!

Bugger.

This isn't working.

How about breaking for lunch?

How about you think about returning to your soap opera days, when you were an English butler? Yes, madam; no, madam; shall I pour the tea now, madam.

Ah . . .

How about we forget that you're a genuine Scots baron from an unnamed Hebrides isle complete with winery and wenches and show you what an unemployment line looks like?

Ah . . .

How about I tell your mother where you are so her paid Highland assassins can pop you off as messily as they like and allow her to sell the winery, the village, the island, and the title, and cavort for the rest of her days in the fleshpots of the Riviera?

• • •

The city, thought Kent Montana—

Not yet, you idiot! You have to wait until I say "Action!"

I think, from the looks of it, that the only action I'm going to get around this damn place is from that woman down at the end of the block.

Careful, Kent. That's your co-star.

You're kidding. But that's . . . that's . . .

That's right. And she still has the porn tape with the Glenn Miller and reggae soundtrack.

The city—

Damnit!

Lionel, Lionel, Lionel.

Kent.

Lionel, allow me, if you will, to remind you that if we don't get started on this epic pretty soon, not only will the audience leave in a huff, demand their money back, and therefore never find out about the mysterious refrigerator in the basement or the antique mummy case in the attic, but I will also not get my own production company. Which means that you will be out of a job. Which means whatever the hell it means when you're out of a job, I wouldn't know about that, I'm too rich.

Kent.

Lionel.

(*dramatic pause*)

Action!

– II –

Soap Flakes

•1•

Kent Montana sat at a quiet window table in the dining room of the Gutted Oyster Lounge, looked out at the street, and thought:

Ah, the city.

And burped.

He winced, touched fastidiously at his lips with his linen napkin, and silently apologized to the world at large for the gastronomical indiscretion. There was no sense apologizing to anybody in the dining room because there wasn't anybody in the dining room. He had been alone when he walked in, he had been alone while he ate, and he was alone now.

I am, he thought miserably and awash in a tepid sea of self-pity, a lonely boy. Then he noticed the back of his right hand, and the stains the blueberry pie had left when it had dribbled down the length of his fork. Lonely and blue, he amended, and scrubbed his skin with the napkin; I'm all alone, with nothing to do.

Damn.

Unfortunately the basis of his solitary lamentation was a lie.

Actually, the alone part wasn't a lie, unless you counted the people on the street, which he didn't, because there weren't any; but the nothing to do part was. He had plenty to do. He just didn't want to do it.

He burped a second time, more of a rolling gurgle, and glared at the tall glass of scotch sitting innocently before him; then he glared at the plate which had, until recently, held an intriguing steak-and-potatoes dinner, which hadn't been half bad, except that the lima beans had tasted like peas and the corn had tasted like lima beans, and even looked like them a little; then he glanced at the salad bowl which, until recently, held green and red and yellow leafy things that may have been nutritious for cattle but would have killed a rabbit on the spot; then he glared at the water glass because there was nothing else to glare at.

Nothing confessed to his gastric upset.

He burped yet a third time.

And once again, which was getting to be too damn many times for his taste, he was forced by circumstance to consider the possibility of omens and portents and other things that tended to lend drama and misery to his life. He never, but never, burped, at least not in public and certainly not after sipping at a reasonable scotch, even if he had been at it for an hour or so. Although the lima beans might have had something to do with it. Which meant, invariably, that something, somewhere, for some reason or other, was telling him that thinking wistfully about being in the city wasn't going to get him there. Not now. Not ever. Instead, the omens hinted with winks broad enough to dislocate an eye socket that he ought to be bloody damn grateful he'd been granted the fabled opportunity of a lifetime, that one chance in a million, that brass ring, that miraculously successful draw to an inside straight, that golden break every actor yearns for and so few are given.

For right now, nestled safely in his suitcase resting against the wall beneath the window, was an imposing manila envelope. In that imposing manila envelope was an imposingly bewildering series of signed and sealed legal papers. And among those bewildering, signed and sealed, imposing legal papers was the incontrovertible, unassailable, and unimpeachable ownership of Stellar Artists Productions, Limited.

His own film company.

Not weekend snaps of Aunt Ida standing in front of Grant's Tomb and smiling as if she knew something Grant didn't.

No.

Film.

As in *movies.*

Good lord, Kent, you should be celebrating your freedom, man; you should be dancing on the tables, laughing in the streets, calling that pea-brain director who fired you from *Passions and Power* and firing him from a job he didn't even know he had; you should be ecstatic, you idiot.

Just imagine: the absolute, complete freedom to choose your own scripts, handpick your own director, privately interview the actresses who will appear on that magic silver screen beside you, decide which exotic locations you'll visit next, never have to wear butler's livery again.

Imagine it.

He did.

He drank and sighed.

He drank and glared, this time at nothing in particular.

He decided that ingratitude had nothing to do with his current disposition, that he had every right to glare, and to burp, because Stellar Artists Productions, Limited, was not, if one were to be honest about it, precisely his. Not really. Only kind of. In a vague, legalistic sort of way. And all those dreams were only dreams because dreaming was the only way he was going to take final possession of the company since taking final possession of the company, which was his only in a phantasmic dreamlike kind of way, involved a catch.

There was, he had learned, always a catch when it came to grabbing that fabled brass ring.

As the old Highland saying goes: Life has catches, then your hair falls in batches.

Words, he thought glumly, to live by.

In general terms, the catch was Hamtucket, Rhode Island, a small community in a small valley in the small state's small western hills. It wasn't an absolutely horrid place, as horrid places go; yet neither was it a thriving and boisterous town on the verge of exploding into a larger town that might even, given time and a professional baseball team, become a small city. It was neither ugly nor beautiful, rich nor poor, plain nor fancy.

What it was, was depressing as hell.

Calling it drab would make it seem too bright. Labeling it melancholy would assume there were parties in the streets every night. Characterizing it as ordinary would give luster to crab grass.

He sighed.

He sipped his scotch.

He gazed forlornly out the window and squinted as the sun blared from behind a cloud, reflecting off the shop windows across the way. The clapboard building's high stone foundation allowed him and the other diners, except there weren't any, to look down at the pedestrians, except there still weren't any. And precious little vehicular traffic either. The stores were open, but in the time he'd been sitting here, alone, and blue, he'd not seen more than a handful of customers enter and leave. An empty school bus rattled southward. A hearse prowled northward. A dog and a cat wandered past side by side, heads inclined toward each other as if they were gossiping.

Marvelous, he thought.

From the bar, which was situated on the other side of the entrance hall and which he had checked and discovered was as empty as the dining room, came the strains of an organ. A solemn organ. An ominous organ that tickled his memory but refused to let him smile.

Right, he thought; and in thinking, considered the specific terms of the catch, as opposed to Hamtucket, which wasn't all that much better but at least it had a highway exit.

The specific was . . . the house.

More specific than that was the time to be spent in . . . the house.

Generally speaking, it wasn't a lot of time, to be sure, but in specific terms it was too long by half

To wit, although there was nothing funny about it: in order to gain final and despotic control of Stellar Artists Productions, Limited, he had to spend one entire night in the domicile that used to belong to Mr. Howmaster Maclemmon. The past tense was particularly relevant here since Maclemmon was dead. More specifically, he had dropped dead of a heart attack in the middle of the street in the middle of the night on the night after his hair had turned white overnight.

The organ trembled softly.

Unconsciously, Kent brushed a hand through his own, embarrassingly abundant, albeit quiet, ginger hair, and sighed his relief when none of it came out in batches.

Howmaster Maclemmon.

The conniving son of a bitch, rest his soul.

Crook, thief, consummate con man, and fairly decent amateur astronomer. He had bilked Kent out of several thousand pounds several times during their long and stormy acquaintanceship, and had been terribly nasty about it whenever Kent had demanded his money back, which was pretty much all the time.

But worse than that, the man never forgave. Anything. Evidently, if one were to consider the will and its diabolical stipulations, certainly not the time Kent had done a little bilking of his own, the consequence of which was Maclemmon's hasty flight to Belgium from the United Kingdom on a Spanish shrimp boat in the middle of January's worst Channel storm since 1687.

At the time, revenge had been sweet; now it tasted like stale sweat socks.

Thus, when Kent had been informed of the inheritance, and its diabolical stipulations, he could not help but wonder if this was but one last-gasp attempt by Howie the prick to get even.

Jesus; spend sunset until dawn in . . . the house . . . or lose it all to . . . the city of Albuquerque.

What the hell kind of a will was that?

The organ muttered a rippling foreboding.

He grunted.

That's what I figured.

And while we're at it, what the hell was Maclemmon doing in Hamtucket anyway? What was so special about this out-of-the-way place that he would hide here from the eyes of the world and my wrath? What was so wonderful about all this gloom that Maclemmon would revel in its despondent ambiance? What was there about the air that had done such terrible things to his hair?

Ah well, he thought; these and other questions will no doubt be answered before this thing is through.

Because, by God, he fully intended to spend that ridiculous night in the house.

Nothing, but nothing, was going to stop him from achieving his practically lifelong dream of artistic independence.

He nodded resolutely, and in nodding saw a woman enter the dining room, saw her see him, and saw her reaction, which made him wonder if his hair was falling out.

When she approached, he rose.

When she said, "Baron? Your lordship?" he nodded.

When she said, "You're going to die if you stay in that house tonight," he dropped back into his chair and finished his scotch, looked out the window and watched the cat bite the dog, the dog whirl in rage and bite a pudgy postman, the pudgy postman lash out with a boot, miss the dog, and fall into the gutter where a towheaded newsboy on a bicycle ran over his right hand, sending the towheaded newsboy into a wild spin that slammed him into the side of a bread van which jumped the curb and slammed into the window of Samson's Video Bazaar.

Kent sniffed and raised an *uh-oh* baronial eyebrow.

Without invitation, the woman sat down.

As she set a formidable-looking purse on the table, he noted that she was rather attractive in a gloomy sort of way, wearing a severe brown suit with padded shoulders, a pale yellow blouse with ruffles that didn't, and her long brown hair in a loose gathering at her nape.

Her pleasantly rounded face seemed puzzled for a moment. "I'm sorry, but . . . you are Kent Montana, are you not?"

Warily he nodded.

She held out a long-fingered hand. "Hester Kerwin."

He shook it politely, although he permitted his expression to tell her that he hadn't the faintest idea who she was, no offense, madam, and you can let go now, please, you've a grip like a bleedin' stevedore.

She flushed slightly and withdrew her hand.

"Perhaps," she answered hastily, "I should explain my warning."

Perhaps, the set of his lips told her, you should.

After checking to be sure no one in the empty room could overhear, she leaned forward and whispered, "Bog-Muggoth."

He waited, hoping her condition wasn't permanent.

She leaned back and waited.

He waited patiently, since barons were pretty good at that sort of thing. They were also pretty good at remembering faces, and although he had never met this woman before, there was something familiar about her. If he could put his finger on it, she'd probably slap him across the room, yet there was . . . something. Her accent, perhaps? Rhode Island, to be sure, but with a trace of—

She leaned forward again, gnawed anxiously at her lower lip, and wrinkled her nose. "Kthulkucuth," she husked skillfully, although she did spit a little.

He waited.

She wiped her chin with a napkin, leaned back, and waited.

The organ sounded downright funereal.

Finally, with her face twisted in mild confusion, she leaned forward a third time. "Do you . . . that is, do you speak English?"

Kent's eyes widened haughtily at the implied insult to the education of his world travels.

She in turn glanced hopelessly around the room. "My god, he doesn't speak English. Wonderful. What the hell am I going to do now?" She looked back at him. "But if you don't speak English, why am I wasting my time talking to you? Why don't I just take the damn thing and leave?"

"Because," he answered softly, "I'll break your arm if you do. What thing?"

She gaped.

He grinned. God, he loved being inscrutable.

She said, "Why the hell didn't you answer me before?"

"Because I didn't understand one bloody word of what you were saying."

"But I was speaking English! I was! You heard me." She glanced down at her lap. "I was, I think, wasn't I? I'm pretty sure I was." She looked up. "I was." She nodded sharply. "Yes, I'm fairly sure I was."

"No, you weren't."

"I wasn't?"

He picked up his spoon and rapped it once on the table. "No, Miss Kerwin, you were speaking in some no doubt arcane, extinct, incomprehensible language, something about bugs and klutzes and things like that."

"Damn," she muttered. "I was so sure I was speaking English, no kidding." She shook her head again, reached into her purse, and fumbled out a dozen audio tape cassettes which, he noted, were part of an extensive multilingual language course for use in an automobile or in the privacy of your own home. There was also a gun, which was a lot more impressive. "Oh, the hell with it, Montana, just give me the damn key."

"What?"

She blinked. "Damn." Though the gun didn't waver, her expression did. "Was that in English, what I just said?"

He nodded.

"Thank god." She brushed the cassettes aside with her free hand. "These things are so confusing sometimes. I—" A frown. "So what did you say 'what' for?"

"Because you pointed a gun at me, asked me for a key, and I was so startled that I wanted to be sure that what you wanted was what you said you wanted."

"The key."

He nodded.

"Okay. Good. Give it to me."

"And if I don't?"

"The key," she said flatly.

"My dear," Kent began, and shut up when she jabbed the gun at him.

At that moment, the waitress, a plump and greying woman in a black dress and red apron, black support hose and shoes with heels thick enough for blarney, thumped over to the table. "Why,

Hester," she said, grinning, chewing gum, fussing with her hair and the dozen pencils poking out of it. "Good to see you, dear. You want something?"

"No thanks. I'm working."

Amy Perkins, or so Kent noticed read her name embroidered on a bosom a starving child would kill for, shook her head in mild scolding. "All work, you know, girl, all work." She turned to Kent, who couldn't believe how magnificently she managed to ignore the gun. "Work, work, work. Two days I've known this young woman, all she does is work. Bad for the complexion, you know what I mean? She should settle down, find a nice young man, raise some kids."

"Ma," Hester said, embarrassed but pleased.

The maternal waitress would have none of it. "Now you listen to me, child. This young man here, he's obviously well-bred, you can tell by his hair. Maybe you should get to know him better, if you catch my drift."

"Ma!"

"She's your mother?" Kent asked.

"Good heavens, no, no, no," the waitress laughed. "Everybody calls me Ma, see. I guess it's my motherly nature, you know what I mean?"

Motherly wasn't exactly what Kent had in mind, but considering her size, and the size of those arms rippling with muscles from hefting trays all day, he chose the wiser course and smiled politely instead.

"So," she said, "you want something else?"

He held up the glass.

She pulled a bottle from her voluminous apron, poured him five fingers, and handed the glass back. "Bar's closed," she explained as she noted the refill on her order pad. When the pencil was safely jammed back into her hair, she walked away. Paused. Looked over her shoulder. "You drink too much. Bad for the liver. My late husband, he drank himself to death, you know. Hester, child, talk to him. He won't listen to me, I'm not his mother."

She left the room.

The organ played her out.

Kent blinked. Once. Very, very slowly.

"Hey," Hester said.

He looked.

"The key, remember?" Her lower lip quivered. "I'm very upset. I'll probably kill you without meaning to. Do you understand? Just give me the key."

Making sure that she understood that he wasn't reaching for a weapon, he reached into his trouser pocket and pulled out the set of keys the Boston attorney had given to him at the reading of the will, just after the man had inexplicably crossed himself four times. There were three, and aside from one fashioned in the shape of a leering skeleton, they appeared to him to be perfectly ordinary.

"You know," he said gently, "it would be rather friendly of you, under the circumstances, if you told me why you want this key. It is, after all, my property. Or at least, it fits a lock on my property. Which lock, I don't know because I haven't looked at my property yet." He smiled. "Well, I looked at it, you see, just in passing, I was in a speeding taxi at the time and it was kind of pointed out to me, but I didn't go inside. I'm just assuming there's something in there that unlocks when you put the key into it, if you see what I mean."

She stared at him.

He maintained the smile.

They jumped when voices at the entrance filtered into the room. Three men stood there, speaking softly to the waitress. One was rather tall, with thick grey hair and rugged features; one wasn't so tall, with slicked-back black hair and puffy features; and the last one was short, pudgy, with slicked-back hair and the biggest eyes Kent had ever seen this side of a magnifying glass. Despite the time of day, they wore evening wear; despite the urging of the waitress, they took one look at Kent and Hester, the tall one tipped his top hat, and they left.

Kent wondered.

The waitress shrugged and disappeared into the bar.

Hester poked his arm and said, "You're telling the truth, aren't you? You really don't know what that key is for, do you?"

He thought to ask her about the three men and decided that it was none of his business why they took one look at him and fled. The way things were going, he'd find out soon enough.

Therefore, when Hester repeated her incredulous query about his not knowing anything vital about the key, he said, "Haven't the foggiest."

"You don't know what Maclemmon was up to, do you?"

"Haven't spoken to him in years."

"You don't know about Pilandra and Quentin and Kenilworth and Ivan and Caroline and Rex and Wally and John and Marsha, do you?"

"Rex?"

Her shoulders sagged in defeat, her cheeks puffed as she blew a soft breath and spat a curse after it, and she swept the cassettes wearily back into her purse, sneered at the gun and put it away.

"I've missed something, right?" he asked in a sparkling fit of stupidity he excused only because of his desperate greed for Stellar Artists Productions and because he was, in situations like this, stupid.

"Baron," she answered, "you don't know the half of it."

"Miss Kerwin," he replied, seeing no reason why he shouldn't pursue his stupidity since it seemed inevitable anyway, "perhaps you should explain before we part."

"Part?"

He frowned. "Well . . . yes."

"You mean I'm fired?"

"You are?"

"You mean you don't want me?"

Courage, Kent, he ordered; courage.

"Fired," she said to the empty room. "He doesn't even know what I can do, and he fires me."

Courage.

"It was the gun, wasn't it?" she decided, snapping her fingers. "You're pissed because of the gun." She slapped the heel of her hand against her brow. "I knew it. I just don't think, you know? Sometimes I just . . . act. Impulses. Instincts. Uncontrollable fancies. You have no idea the trouble I get into sometimes."

Kent smiled. Painfully. "Miss Kerwin—"

"Fired," she muttered, and a tear shimmered in one eye before she brushed it away with the side of her thumb.

"You are not fired," he answered impetuously, and crossed his fingers under the table.

"I'm not?"

"No. Why should you be?"

"Because you said we were parting."

"But aren't we?"

"Not if I'm not fired."

"But you're not."

"Then we're not parting."

"We're not?"

"Am I fired?"

"Not so's I notice."

She grinned. "Good." She stood. "Glad that's settled." She stepped away from the table. "Let's go, Baron. I'll tell you all about Caroline and Wally and Ivan and Quentin and Rex and Pilandra and Kenilworth and John and Marsha on the way."

"Rex?"

She pulled him to his feet, patted his arm, and led him to the door. "You won't regret it, believe me."

He stopped. "Miss Kerwin."

"Pushy, right?" she said immediately. "Too pushy. Headstrong. Reactive."

He put a finger to her lips, not incidentally noting they were much softer than they looked. "Miss Kerwin. Hester. Who, if you don't mind me asking, the hell are you?"

"Didn't the lawyer tell you?"

He shook his head.

"Hell, Baron, I'm your housekeeper."

"Ah."

She shrugged. "At least I will be until you're dead."

✦2✦

Hamtucket boasted many grim and dismal streets among those streets that performed the function of connecting one street to another unless you cut through someone's back yard. Most of the homes were inhabited by shopkeepers and artisans whose livelihoods had been slowly, inexorably eroded by the disastrous failure of the ice cream factory two decades before, and the unexpected collapse of the burgeoning boa and boater businesses which had, in their burgeoning, kept half of Boston and most of Hartford at the pinnacle of fashion awareness. But the boas bombed under constricting charges of destructive featherbedding, the boaters sank without a tip, and the ice cream melted when the refrigerator blew out, killing four men, including the foreman; and the workers, try as they might, couldn't find other employment unless they commuted to Providence and Newport.

Houses fell into genteel disrepair; stores held more sales and made less profit; children grew up and moved away; adults moved away and returned when they couldn't find employment in Providence and Newport; schools closed; the police force was reduced because crime had been reduced by the absence of anything marginally worth stealing.

It was, in a word, pretty bad times.

Times of decay and dissolution, of desperation and despair, and much of it, although not all of it since some people were too rich to worry about depression, could be found on the typical street known as Langford Place.

Most of the houses were large, most of them were Victorian, and all were proud. The small lawns were assiduously tended through drought and hurricane, the peeling paint was trimmed to give that elegantly mottled dowager look, the trees died gracefully and without much fuss except for the one that fell on the Mayor three years ago, and the small park at the end of the block became a symbol of all that once was, and all that would never be again.

It would have been sad if it didn't look so godawful.

And it was to this place of despair and economic distress that Kent Montana walked with his housekeeper, Hester Kerwin, as the October sun set over Connecticut, a patchy mist sifted down from the surrounding hills, and the Red Sox blew yet another World Series.

This then was Hamtucket, on . . .

. . . the edge of night.

3

Kent paused at the mouth of Langford Place, unable to shake the feeling, and a dreadfully familiar one it was, that what he was about to do had not quite been done by him before, but it was coming awfully close, and if he had any brains at all, he would turn around immediately and walk away into the sunset before the sun set and it was too dark to see anything, much less where he was going.

It was, as was his fate as a man cursed to fall into mud and come up smelling muddy, a dilemma.

But he was here; so, for the time being, he might as well make the best of it. Who knows? The dilemma, however one defined it, may resolve itself without his having to do anything, in which case he was worrying over nothing; and if he had to do something, he was fairly sure he'd be able to do the proper thing without getting himself killed. And if he got himself killed, there was nothing to worry about anyway, so why worry.

He frowned.

He sniffed.

He adjusted his tailored denim windbreaker more snugly across his shoulders and ignored the little voice that told him his logic had more holes in it than the black lace shawl he had once seen on a New Orleans stripper. Voices like that only tended to confuse him.

Instead, he focused his concentration on the pale mist drifting in writhing patches through the leafless trees and lifeless air; he saw the houses drifting stoically through time; he felt the damp chill of the autumn twilight breeze, heard a dog barking listlessly in someone's home, saw a cat prowling importantly around some fairly impressive hedges; he noted the way the street parted at the far end to enclose a small park and fill it with shadows; he wasn't sure because it was getting so dark so fast, but he was fairly positive he saw telescopes affixed to many of the peaks of slanting slate roofs.

Meanwhile, Hester, haltingly and in oddly accented English, explained about Ivan and Pilandra and Quentin and Caroline and John and Kenilworth and Wally and Rex and Marsha.

She told him so much in so short a time, in fact, that he began to have another one of those feelings, this one of the kind that suggested he had missed far too many episodes to be able to catch up in one night.

Oh god, he thought in sudden panic; please, no.

As they continued on down the street, slowly, their footsteps echoing faintly, he glanced into a sloping yard dominated by a magnificent if somewhat rotted oak tree with a bald tire swing hanging from a single stout branch, and to his astonishment spotted a proud spark of artistic zest encompassed in a small ivory statue of a radio dial from another era, when the tide of time took its time coming in, bringing with it all the nautical cheer of a life buoy ringing gaily on the horizon.

Oh no, he thought with a shiver of horrified premonition that took over from the sudden panic; oh lord, no.

He stopped again.

Ivan. Caroline. Quentin. Rex? John. The others. All of them with missions, all of them with joys and sins and woes and houses.

All of them with . . . secrets.

He made a face at the moon he couldn't see through all the mist. God damn, I *knew* there was something familiar about all this.

He looked to Hester then, who looked back, saw his expression of dismayed recognition, and nodded wisely with a small sad smile and a consoling pat to his hand.

The organ rippled.

The dog barked.

The cat howled.

"Well, at least," he said sourly, "I'm not a butler this time."

She frowned.

"Never mind." He took her arm, thrust out his chin, and straightened his spine. "Lead on, Miss Kerwin, lead on. Take me to my midnight home so I can get the hell out of here first thing in the morning."

She opened her mouth.

He closed it with a scowl. "Nothing," he warned with an upraised finger. "Say nothing, Miss Kerwin, about dying, killing, or losing one's life. Not only is it self-defeating, it makes me nervous."

"Your funeral," she muttered.

He chuckled at her curiously endearing, and maddeningly familiar, dour demeanor. "Hester, there are some things in life, you'll learn soon enough, which are, unless you can duck them, unavoidable. Know this, lass, and know it well: I fully intend to comply with Howmaster's batty conditions and come out of it smelling like a rose."

"Lilies," she countered sourly.

"Only," he said, pointing, "if that's the place I have to stay in. God, what a monstrosity."

And as soon as he said it he knew it was a mistake. Stupid is, he thought glumly, as stupid does.

The strange high house in the mist was strange. It was narrow, high, and virtually paintless; all the narrow windows on the second floor and attic had been boarded over; the slate roof sagged, the porch sagged, the crooked front walk was of concrete that must have been poured in Hadrian's time, the shallow lawn was hardy weeds shot through with browning grass, the driveway was more accurately a footpath to a garage in back that was more like a shack, and the wrought iron numbers nailed to the flat porch roof over the steps were so rusted that the last of daylight flared off them red.

668, as if in pulsing clotting blood.

It reminded him of the summer home in the North Sea his mother had brought him to when he was eleven, just before she handed him over to the Holy Sisters of Benevolent Persecution on the shores of Loch Ness. That place—the summer house, not the abbey, although that had been bad enough, what with the moat, loaded pious cannon, and all—had been much like this place, which is to say foreboding, forbidding, unsavory, and filled with so many traps of a lethal orientation that he had survived only because he was fleet of foot, quick of mind, and she'd forgotten most of the ammunition.

Ah well, he decided, it could be worse.

He thought a little longer and noted the lovingly cared for Cape Cod immediately to the left, the dignified restored Queen Anne to the right.

Maybe not.

Suddenly Hester grabbed his elbow before he could take that first fatal step up the walk of no return until tomorrow morning. "You don't have to do this," she urged, her gaze searching his face for signs of latent intelligence. "Really. You don't. I mean, you're rich, right? Wealthy. Affluent. A man of means. You could buy your own stupid film company, you don't need this one. Start one if you can't buy one. What do you want one for anyway?"

"I am an actor," he declared proudly, not bothering to mention the greed, the power, the private interviews.

"Well, you're a baron, too," she reminded him. "Wealthy. Affluent. I said that already. Did I? Yes. I'm sure I did. And damnit, it was in English, I know it was. Anyway, do you think

Lord Olivier would do something foolish like this just to get his own film company?"

Kent smiled tolerantly. "He's dead."

She looked at him.

The innocence he gave her was the best he could do with the line he'd been fed.

"You're not going to change your mind?"

"No," he said firmly.

"You sure?" she asked, fiddling with her ruffles.

"Absolutely," he responded, averting his face from her alluring temptation.

Time passed.

Finally, with a resigned sigh and severely pursed lips, she snatched the keys from his hand, shook her head at the folly of a man who dressed pretty good but was a jerk nonetheless, and headed for the door.

As she moved away, a cloud of mist suspiciously like more fog thickened over the empty silent street, engulfed it, smothered it, muffled it, but not before Kent spotted a solitary hunched figure moving swiftly and clumsily through the evening several yards distant; oddly enough, it was cowled, and the rustle of its dark, monklike robes sifted through the night like the hissing of a sleepy serpent.

He rubbed his eyes, and the figure vanished.

He stared, and the figure did not reappear.

All right, he thought; that's all right. Monks are a good sign. Men of God, and all that. Unless it's Rasputin. But he's dead. So it's a good sign. Besides, he's too short.

At the same time, however, he noted with an actor's keen observation that few of the other homes were lighted for the evening. And those that were had all their draperies drawn, their shades down, and, no doubt, their doors locked and bolted.

Are we that alone? he wondered.

Suddenly the sound of a modern key in an ancient lock shrieked painfully through the neighborhood; a second later, the sound of a door badly in need of oil shrieked eerily through the neighborhood; shortly after that, the sudden glow of a switched-on light chased the shadows into corners where they sneered and snickered.

And Kent realized then that the fateful moment he had been dreading and waiting for and hating and anticipating had finally arrived.

Last chance, man, he told himself as he took a deep calming breath; you can leave now, no one will ever know, and you can lie through your teeth to the lawyer in the morning. You could. You really could.

"Hey, Baron!" Hester called, a mere sensuous shadow in the doorway. "You going to stand there all night, or are you coming in? I'm cold."

Nuts.

A sudden noise behind him then; a scraping, a rasping, a quite very good sneaking up on him except for the noise.

Suddenly, before he could move:

"Be . . . ware."

He closed his eyes tightly, clenched his fists until they were bloodless, and did his level best not to scream; he had some standards after all. Then, when he had assured himself that his heart had not been too badly damaged when it had slammed against the back of his teeth, he turned slowly.

A scrawny little man with a four-day beard, a moth-eaten cloth cap, and not quite ragged clothes stood on the curb. He was carrying an ironing board.

"Did you say something?" Kent asked, so carefully neutral that he almost choked himself. If this was one of his mother's hired assassins, things weren't going so well back home.

The man nodded solemnly. "Be . . . ware." His voice was whiskey rough, and his breath, even at this distance, wasn't all that smooth either.

Kent's conscience warned him, his instincts were damn near hysterical, but he said it anyway because it was that kind of night: "Beware of what?"

The little man coughed dryly into a half-gloved fist, then pointed a long, bony, grimy finger at him. "Be . . . ware the Ides of March."

Kent nodded. "Right."

The man's gratified smile revealed a silver tooth.

"It's October."

The little man leaned back. "Never!"

Kent crossed his heart.

The little man drew himself up haughtily and thrust not much of a chin ahead of him. "That's im— . . . I am never . . . are you sure?"

Kent, who had noticed that the scruffy fellow had a discernible

Russian accent, allowed as how he was fairly sure that, since last month was September, this month was truly October and, he added quickly, the Ides of October had been almost a fortnight ago.

The little Russian took off his cap, scratched through a disreputable thatch of greying hair, snarled when something bit him, slapped his scalp lustily several times, and replaced the cap. "Very well," he said. "I . . . very well."

After a slight bow of apology, he walked off across the street, dragging the ironing board behind him.

Kent watched him vanish into the dark and the mist suspiciously like a fog. He made no attempt to give chase. Stupid was one thing; out of his effing mind was something else. Instead he turned up the walk straightaway, climbed the porch steps, and smiled wanly at the housekeeper. "Nice neighborhood," he remarked.

And then he said, "Jesus Christ, woman, where the hell's all the furniture?"

✦4✦

Meanwhile . . .

There wasn't much to do this time of year in Langford Place Park except look at some naked trees and dead flowers, sit on the handful of concrete benches, or throw coins in the fountain. Nobody did any of it. The flora was disgusting even when it was alive, the benches were cold, and the fountain, carved from imported Dakota marble in urban ugly, was a waist-high chipped bowl fifteen feet in diameter, with a winged woman standing in the center, holding an elaborate vase from which water dribbled every once in a while.

The woman may have been an angel, but Caroline Putney thought she was probably a slut, or a close friend of the sculptor. No angel she ever saw ever had a figure like that, or lips like that, or a look in her eye so suggestive as to make the pigeons multiply and, in season, be fruitful.

She turned away in proper disgust and walked slowly toward the north exit. Rex wasn't here. She could see that. At least, he wasn't in the parts that weren't too dark to see him if he was in them. And not only wasn't he here, it didn't look as if he was going to be here. And if he wasn't going to be here, then Wally probably would be here since it was getting on toward that time when the dog needed its exercise before dinner.

She fretted. Her fingers snapped nervously, her long blonde hair caught in the chilly breeze and tangled attractively, her huge blue eyes scanned the bushes, the benches, and the trees hopefully, and her topcoat flapped provocatively about her long slender legs. She considered leaving the park and going home so that Wally would suspect nothing. But if she left, she might miss Rex, who would miss her if he arrived and she wasn't here, waiting, since she was the one who had called him earlier in such a bewildered panic that he had immediately suggested this daring, almost daylight meeting.

Oh lord, lord, she thought, what I wouldn't give not to be such a lustful, free-spirited, unencumbered by bourgeois morals woman!

For after all, wasn't it simple lust that drove her into Rex's manly arms time after time after time after time? Wasn't it the lack of true spiritual love that sent her to Wally's lumpy mattress twice a week and once extra on holidays, although summers were kind of sporadic because she got so sweaty? Wasn't that her fatal character flaw that had the jealous spinsters of Hamtucket gossiping maliciously about her?

Not that she gave a damn.

Lust, for one thing, meant never having to say you're sorry; for another, it meant being sorry didn't matter anyway, which was, in the long run, a good thing, since lust could really stir up the old guilt if you were sorry you were lustful, which, since it was lust, meant that you weren't.

It was, when she thought about it, so terribly tidy, wasn't it?

Yet these, and other questions, bothered her less tonight than the unmitigated horror she had discovered only two days ago, the horror she had to share with Rex because Wally thought she was losing her mind.

She looked apprehensively up the street, into the deepening mist, listening for Rex's comforting footsteps, that tell-tale cute little clip-clop limp which was the result of an heroic accident on a dude ranch in Wyoming all those many years ago. But she heard nothing, saw nothing, felt nothing but the mist gathering sensuously on her high cheekbones and across her velvety brow.

Perhaps, she thought, I should just buckle down and be plucky and save everyone myself. It wouldn't be as much fun, of course. Her hair would get mussed, for one thing; for another, all those designer clothes Wally had bought for her in Hartford would get wrinkled. Still, if push came to shove and it was a matter between life and death, some hard choices would have to be made before the night was over.

She sighed.

She looked over her shoulder, and gasped.

Someone stood enigmatically by the fountain. A man. A tall man in a white linen shirt, jodhpurs, and gleaming riding boots, his long blond hair all attractively atangle in the fitful night breeze.

She clamped a hand over her heart to confine its wild, lustful beating; she took a deep breath lest she faint dead away and ruin her hose; she took a tentative step forward and whispered "Rex?" before breaking into a run that soon had her nestling in his arms.

"Caroline!"

"Rex!"

"Oh, Caroline!"

"Oh, Rex!"

She smiled into his glinting blue eyes.

He raised an eyebrow and smiled into her melting aqua orbs.

"Rex," she whispered.

"Caroline," he husked.

Sensing an imminent interlude which might distract her from her purpose, she disentangled herself regretfully from his manly embrace, took his hand, and led him to the exit. There, panting enchantingly, she pointed toward the middle of the west side of the block.

"Rex," she confided solemnly.

He frowned, brushed a hand through the air as though to banish the gathering mist, and said, "Caroline?"

She nodded.

He appeared to be in shock.

She didn't know what to say, how to convey her feelings of terror and impending misfortune, how to convince him that she wasn't imagining things and that, truly, their lives were in mortal danger if they appeared at that dinner this evening.

"Caroline," he said, cautioning her not to jump to conclusions.

Her answer was a quick tug of his hand, pulling him into the concealing shadow of a weeping willow, then pointing at the figure of a man stepping out of the mist. A man, she noted instantly, of obvious breeding, with a slightly squared jaw, an aristocratic aura, and enough hair to make her legs wobble with illicit desire. She steadied herself lest Rex notice and watched as the man handed something to that horridly common Hester Kerwin—who had bigger breasts than she did, the bitch—who eventually frumped up the walk and unlocked the, door.

Of the house.

That house.

Then the aristocratic man turned suddenly, cocked his head with all that lovely hair, and began speaking to another man who had materialized out of the mist.

"Vlaskovich," Rex grumbled distastefully.

She nodded knowingly. For it was indeed Ivan Vlaskovich, the neighborhood seer and Hamtucket town drunk who, she had recently learned from that horridly large waitress at the Gutted Oyster, was actually a displaced Russian peasant who had fled his native land with his precious ironing board in order to find a new life in the New World. No one trusted him. His clothes were always wrinkled.

When the two men parted, Caroline could not believe that the stranger actually went up the steps. That he actually listened to something that disgusting housekeeper person called to him. That he . . . she fell against Rex's arm in disbelief and severe trepidation.

Manfully Rex steadied her with a grunt and a thrust of his more squared than the stranger's chin before stepping out into the open, his lips parted to call a warning.

"Oh Rex!" she cried.

It was too late.

A light flooded the stoop, the stairs, and the sidewalk, and the stranger stepped in.

"Oh," she sighed, "Rex."

And the door closed behind him.

The organ hit just the right note.

A cat yowled.

A dog barked.

With a manicured hand pressed lightly to her mouth to smother a startled gasp, she spun around just in time to see Wally sift out of the mist, following the excited tug of a rhinestone leash at the end of which was Puffball, her Rhode Island champion dalmatian. Panic seized her in its cold, deathlike grip, and she whirled around, searching desperately for a place to hide.

Rex was gone.

Puffball barked joyfully.

"Caroline, darling, is that you?" Wally called, his short blond hair feeble in the evening breeze, his watery blue eyes squinting through the mist.

"Oh Wally!" she cried, deciding to brazen it out, what the hell.

But when she saw the tiny cowled figure streak out of the mist and back in again, when she remembered why she was out here in the first place, when she remembered the last words Howmaster Maclemmon had said to her on the night he had died, she also remembered her mother's sage maternal advice about unpleasant confrontations and unnecessary explanations. She fainted; but not before she heard the organ strike eight.

Meanwhile . . .

Dr. Kenilworth Smith was about as ugly as you can get without being a Greek legend with snakes in your hair. But his nature was such that his character made up for just about everything but the snakes. He was seldom without companionship, never without friends, and always had what people assumed was a smile on what they assumed were his lips. One might say he had a rich, full life.

That fateful misty night, however, he was alone. Sitting by the living room window in Number 669. In the dark. On the table beside him was a glass of sipping bourbon, already three times refilled; in his lap was a spiral notebook, most of its lined pages already filled; and in his left hand was a pair of seaman's binoculars, which he placed on the table with a thump and a loud weary sigh.

It was too late.

Too . . . late.

Although he had spotted the stranger at the house directly across the street, he had wasted too much time examining him for signs of Evil and Degradation for him to prevent the man from entering that building at the behest, apparently, of the not unattractive but certainly in need of private medical attention Hester Kerwin. Then he had noted Wally Putney conversing with his wife down by the park, and knew that he dare not show his face lest Caroline give away their guilty secret and force him to leave the Place he called home.

He was trapped, then, in his own abode, helpless to stop the events which had begun with Maclemmon's horrible death and, he was fairly positive, would not end until the entire world had crumbled into stellar dust.

He drank.

He refilled his glass.

He drank.

He picked up his notebook and stared at the words he had written on the last page, scowling because he couldn't read them in the dark but not daring to turn on a light. If he did, the others would know he was home. He wasn't supposed to be home. He was supposed to be at a surgeons' convention in downtown Omaha. If they, his patients, knew he had lied to them about downtown Omaha, what disasters would then befall his thriving practice? What secrets, besides his own, would spill like slick slime into the gutters and befoul the lives of all these wonderful people? What vicious queries would be raised in official circles as a result of his apparent disregard for their innocent trust?

He sighed.

He drank.

These, and other questions, would be answered, he knew, in due time, if only because by dawn, give or take a few hours, the answers would be clear enough.

And he would be ruined.

Dead, too.

Alas, he thought, and fell asleep.

Meanwhile . . .

In Number 697, John Laste stood in front of the bathroom mirror and examined the age lines imprinted upon his face. There seemed to be more of them tonight than there were yesterday, and more yesterday than the day before, and more, if he remembered correctly, than last year at this same time. He leaned closer and touched the mirror lightly with a sharpened pencil, gauged length and distance and average depth, grunted, then made a scientific notation on a hand-drawn facial chart lying on the counter beside the sink. When he was finished, he slapped his cheeks to bring them color, rubbed the heel of a hand across his forehead to smooth out the frown, stood back and proceeded to adjust his silk club tie with the unicorn on the knot.

"Darling?"

His wife, calling from the hall. His wife, standing out there like some kind of humanoid vulture, just waiting to pounce upon the ravages of his corpse. His wife, who would be, he thought with an evilly gratified grin, no longer his wife once this evening was over and Maclemmon kept his promise.

"Yes, darling?" he called back sweetly.

"I'm having trouble with my facial chart."

Just pour ink on it, you old cow, he thought.

"After dinner," he called sympathetically. "We have no time now."

"But I think there's another crow's foot."

He looked at the door. It was open. She was there. Diamonds and pearls and an appropriately subdued black dress with emerald bodice and stockings with seams on the back and stylishly white hair with a feather crawling through the Shirley Temple curls.

"Put your shoes on," he suggested, "and nobody will notice."

She looked down, shook her head, and smiled foolishly. "You know, I thought I was shorter."

He smiled.

She smiled back and walked away.

He looked back at the mirror and finished adjusting his tie. Then he slipped into his evening jacket, kicked off his evening slippers and slipped into his evening shoes, took a brush from the counter and set about working on his lapels, his evening trousers, and his evening shirt.

"Darling?"

He looked at the door. It was open. She was there.

"What it is, Marsha?"

"Do you really think we need a cab?"

"Darling, the Lastes do not walk. The Lastes ride."

"Yes, but—"

He waved her silent. "We neither cook, nor do we sew. We neither toil, nor do we pay taxes. We neither soil, nor are we soiled. It is," he added pointedly, "the way of it, my dear, and I should think that after thirty-five years, you would know that by now."

She pointed a multi-ringed finger. "There's a hair on your shoulder."

He whirled to the mirror. "My god."

"It's a blonde hair," she added.

He said nothing.

"It's Caroline Putney's, isn't it?"

"Don't be ridiculous, it's the cat's," he snarled, plucking the offending hair away with two disgusted fingers and dropping it with an exaggerated grimace into the garbage disposal. He flicked the switch. The hair was ground. He looked to the door. It was still open. She was still there.

"The cat's dead," she said.

"It's an old jacket," he answered.

And then, shockingly and for the first time in ages, he was at a loss for words.

In the doorway. It was her. Rather, it was the look on her face. There was neither sadness there, nor was there acute disappointment; there was neither hurt, nor was there pain; there was neither resignation, nor was there blind, loving, adoring, devotional belief.

No indeed.

Marsha Furst-Laste was very, very annoyed.

Shaken at her uncharacteristic burst of harsh emotion, he returned to the mirror and brushed at the spot where the hair had been before it had been ground. Howie, he thought, if you're not right, I'm a dead man.

Meanwhile . . .

In Number 621, a handsome young man with extraordinarily blond hair paced impatiently in the sparsely furnished living room. He wore what his mother called his Sunday best, and he hated it. Jeans, a sloppy shirt, a good pair of beat-up, foot-fitting sneakers—that was his preferred uniform of whatever day it happened to be; but wearing a suit, especially one with lapels as wide as a jumbo jet's wingspan, was sheer seersucker torture.

"Mom," he complained, "do I really have to go?"

His mother entered the room, smoothing her apron over her plain floral work dress. She was young once, back when she was twenty; now she was middle-age, a lifetime of hard work visible on her reddened hands, on her lean face which had been pretty once and would be pretty again if only she would stop working so hard and think of herself for a change, and in the glints of silver in her raven black hair.

Not, he thought with an abrupt blush of contrition, that she was ugly. She wasn't. She just looked that way sometimes because of all the sacrifices she had made over the years to raise him, the men she had turned down, the laundry she took in four times a week, the carpentry on the side, and that pothole-filling gizmo she kept in the garage where the car used to be when they used to have a car before she had to sell it to buy the pothole-filling gizmo.

"You look nice," she said proudly, wiping her hands on her apron.

"I feel like a jerk."

"It'll be for the best, you'll see."

He jammed his hands into the pockets of trousers that were too large at the butt and sagged at the knees. "I think it's stupid."

"You're young. You'll learn."

"Mom," he said, "I'm not a teenager anymore."

An expression of long-suffering devotion and perseverance crossed her face.

He knew that look, and groaned.

She crossed the threadbare carpet, pulled his hands from his pockets, and said, "Quentin. Son. This is your big chance. Your opportunity to leave this place and make something of yourself The chance your poor late father never had." She brushed a limp strand of hair from her eye. "You shouldn't worry about me. I'll be all right. I don't mind. I've had my life. Now it's time to have yours."

"Mom," he said, "for god's sake, you're not even forty-five yet. God, you could get married again, you know. I wouldn't mind."

She smiled sorrowfully. "No, dear. I don't think so. I already have the man I want."

He frowned at her.

She smiled at him.

He said, "He won't even know me."

"He'll remember."

"Mom," he said, pulling his hands away and turning to the window with the tattered shade. "Mom, I was a corpse, for god's sake."

"He'll remember."

He shook his head. It was so hard trying to be an aspiring actor, so many lines to learn, so many auditions to attend, so many other aspiring actors who kept telling you not to quit your day job while they quit their day jobs and stole your parts from you. The only decent role he had had so far was that of a corpse on something called *Passions and Power.* True, it had lasted for nearly two months and there was no memorization involved, but still, it was hardly the way he'd dreamed of breaking into the limelight.

Since then, practically nothing. A non-speaking role in a summer theater production of *Mark Twain Tonight;* one line in a local drama theater presentation of *Twelve Angry Men;* and another corpse, this time in a re-creation of the Battle of Gettysburg by the river over in Providence. The biggest opportunity since then had been a shot at an independent film being made somewhere down in New jersey. Something about lawyers and giant crayfish taking over New York, with gratuitous naked women. But he had lost that chance when his mother had come down with double pneumonia and creeping bursitis and he couldn't leave her side, not with all those potholes to be filled in and Mrs. Putney's dainties to be laundered. By hand. Lord. If it wasn't for Sheila, he didn't know what he'd do.

"I don't know, Mom," he said wearily. "I really don't know."

She patted his back, adjusted his shoulders, dropped to her knees and, from a pin cushion strapped to her wrist, began working on his trousers so they wouldn't sweep the floor.

He looked down.

She smiled up.

He looked out the window.

He shuddered.

There were secrets out there in that dark October night. He could sense them. He could feel them. Somebody knew something they weren't telling somebody else, and he had a sinking sensation that he was the somebody else. Why else would he receive an invitation to an exclusive dinner party given by a dead man? Why else would he, Quentin Eddye, be asked to be in the company of a great actor like Kent Montana? Why else would everybody on the block practically except him have telescopes nailed to their roofs, telescopes which had been, he had noted with an aspiring actor's young eye, in suspiciously frequent use over the past two weeks—ever since Howmaster Maclemmon had dropped dead right out there in the middle of the street?

His mother finished his trousers and began polishing his shoes.

Ah well, he thought resignedly; these, and other questions no doubt, would be answered before this night was through.

He only wished Sheila would be there.

But she had to stay home, in Number 619, tending her aged father and her unwed, pregnant sister, and her drug-crazed, alcoholic, disreputable brother.

He sighed.

He checked his watch.

One hour, he thought; one more hour before I make a jackass of myself.

His mother pulled a hydro-laundry hand sponge she'd invented from her apron pocket and washed his socks.

"Mother, please!" he snapped uncharacteristically at her loving ministrations. "I'd rather do it myself!"

She sighed and wiped a sacrificial tear from the corner of one eye. "All right, dear, all right," she said, groaning lithely to her feet. "I'll just go get the blow dryer. It's all right. I know where it is. The stairs aren't that high. I can make it." She patted his arm. "You just stand here and look handsome in case somebody walks by."

Caroline Putney walked by.

Quentin swallowed, closed his eyes, and wished that the ground would open up and swallow him; failing that, that his mother would turn her ankle or something so that he could stay home and take care of her.

Anything to keep from going out tonight.

A dog barked.

The organ muttered.

Women cackled.

Someone snored.

And down in the park, the winged marble woman holding the dribbling vase flexed her wings.

Once.

5

The cowled figure opened the door, tripped over the hem of its imported wool robe and fell inside. It rolled instantly onto its back and kicked the door shut with its foot. Then it stared at the ceiling; or it would have stared at the ceiling if it could have seen the ceiling, which it couldn't because there weren't any lights on, so it did the best it could under the circumstances, except that the damn robe kept bunching up between its legs and giving it a thrill not entirely apropos to the situation. And as it sort of stared in the general direction of where the ceiling ought to be, it clasped its hands to its chest in a pattern so intricate only two hands could have formed it.

"Bog-Muggoth," it said.

It said a lot of other things in a sing-song, chanting, praying sort of way, but mostly it said, "Bog-Muggoth."

Once, however, it made a mistake and said, "Kthulkucuth," and spent a frightful ten minutes waiting for the ceiling to fall in, because it wasn't time for that one.

Not yet.

Midnight.

Oh yes, it thought as it rolled to its knees and sat back on its heels; oh yes, midnight.

It giggled.

It laughed.

It stood up and tripped over the hem of its robe, fell, stood up, tore off the robe and turned on the light, tripped over the robe and fell into the living room, where it crawled to the sofa and sat crosslegged on the center cushion.

It sat for an hour in quivering meditation.

A few minutes after that, it said, "Bog-Muggoth," and finally, at long last, after all this time, even though it had known it would happen sooner or later, give or take a year, it felt the *power.*

And it knew.

"They're coming," it whispered to the empty room. "Son of a bitch, they're really coming."

– III –

One Life to Live

◆1◆

The front hall of Number 668 was very nearly square, and not a very large square at that.

On the wall to the left was a tottering narrow staircase to the second floor, the banister looking as if a good sneeze or a hiccup would bring it down; on the right a doorless doorway led into what Kent saw was a front parlor connected to a back parlor by a large, equally open archway. Straight ahead was a small dining room, and in back was a kitchen with a glass-paned door leading to a filthy mud porch. It didn't take long to explore all the rooms; there was nothing to distract him. No chairs, no couches, no bookcases, no tables. Nothing hung from the walls whose ancient floral wallpaper was cracked and stained and faded in places where the sun struck it during the day; there was but one bulb in the diamond-shaped dining room chandelier, one bulb in the kitchen's tomato-shaped chandelier, two bulbs in the back parlor chandelier shaped like a cultured pearl, zilch in the hall, and a flashlight resting on the first step up. Instead of draperies, there were ratty black-out shades on all the tall narrow windows. The floors were bare, scuffed hardwood rapidly aspiring to sponge.

"I am," Kent said fatalistically, "supposed to spend the night here."

The housekeeper, who had been following him silently throughout his tour, nodded.

"I am," he continued, "supposed to sleep on the floor."

"The upstairs isn't any better, if you've been hoping," she told him.

He had been. He sighed. Then he frowned. "If you're the housekeeper, what have you been keeping?"

"The house, what else?"

As he wandered helplessly, hopelessly, miserably, into the back parlor and peered into the small fireplace mouth on the lefthand wall, he also noted that there were cobwebs in the high corners, colonies of dust bunnies gathering to emigrate along the baseboards, and unidentifiable grey things clinging hypnotically to ceilings more cracked than his mother. The fireplace itself hadn't been used in so long there were scattered traces of birds' nests that had filtered down through the flue, along with a couple of feathers that appeared to be petrified.

"When," he asked out of idle and insane curiosity, "did you start work?"

"Two days ago," she answered promptly. "And I want you to know that I don't do windows."

Among other things, he thought uncharitably.

Then she reached into a doorless closet beside the fireplace and pulled out some rickety, and appallingly small, folding chairs with slatted backs and seats with smiling robins and chickadees with halos stenciled on them. Then she promptly began unfolding them with a snap of a wrist here and a kick of one thick-soled shoe there. He stood on the slate hearth out of her way and watched in silent incredulity as she arranged the tiny chairs around the perimeter of the room, snarling at the stubborn ones, replacing a slat on another, all the while complaining that Sunday schools just didn't have the goods anymore these days, especially at the rental rates they had the Christian nerve to charge. She fussed, she readjusted, she nudged, she stood back and scowled, she nudged again, and finally nodded her approval.

"Interesting," he said.

She smiled. "Thank you. It isn't much, but it'll have to do. They told me I would have to make do. I think I did. Do you think I did?"

"I think so. For what?"

"For what?"

He nodded.

"The scumbag didn't tell you?"

He shook his head.

Her hands slapped her legs in exasperation. "Great." She walked to the window and pulled the shade aside, peering into the night. "Great."

As best he could, Kent maintained his aristocratic poise as he flopped onto a chair, nearly toppled backward, found his balance, crossed his legs, and watched a spider vanish into a crack in the floorboards. As spiders go, it wasn't very large, but before it disappeared, he couldn't help noticing that it was a bright, virtually neon, green. Now, spiders, as he recalled from his days with the Holy Sisters, were generally not neon green, not even in the Amazon where things existed that didn't dare exist anywhere else because otherwise people would either kill them or be dead.

They were definitely not neon green in Rhode Island.

And he, of course, had to sleep on the floor.

Swell.

Hester rattled the shade in agitation, shook her head, and muttered to herself

From his position so close to the floorboards he might as well be directly on them, Kent found himself looking straight at the back of her knees. They were dimpled. They were . . . attractive. And when she turned with a wet sound of disgust, he realized that the fronts of them weren't all that bad either. Accordingly, and without a twinge, twang, or tweak of conscience, he followed close behind his gaze as it traveled up the rest of her front until he gazed into her eyes, which were trying to appear stern and flattered and insulted simultaneously. It made her cross-eyed.

"Checking on the neighbors, were we?" was the only thing he could think of to say if he wasn't going to say something so terminally inane that she'd slap his cheek onto the anvil of his ear and pound him a good one.

What he didn't expect was the way her mouth opened and her face paled alarmingly.

"Why did you say that?" she demanded, stomping across the floor. "Damnit, what made you say that?"

To save his neck from snapping, he lowered his head and found her knees again. Quite nice, actually.

"I must have been delirious," he confessed. "The shock of a friend's death and all that."

"Bullshit. What do you know about the neighbors?"

"Nothing. I just moved in, remember? I don't even know what the capital of Rhode Island is." He imagined that her left knee had grown a mouth. Amazing.

"Providence, and why do you think I was looking over there?"

"I . . . don't know."

She slapped her thighs in resentment of the role thrust upon her. "He didn't tell you that, either, did he? The scumbag. The shyster. The ambulance chaser. The bloodsucker. He never said anything about anything to you, did he?"

Amazing. The knee actually sounded like her.

"Well, did he?"

"No," he admitted. "I was notified of the will. I showed up at the office. In Boston, as a matter of fact. He gave me the papers. I signed them. He signed them. We shook hands. I left and came here straightaway. On a coach, mind you." He squinted at the memory, and his upper lip curled. "You know, the driver never even came to a full stop. He just opened the door, tossed out my bag, told me to mind my step when he pushed me off, and left." The squint narrowed, and he scratched behind one ear. "Damn, I must be getting slow."

"Oh great. You know, I don't like things that don't work the way they should. He should have told you, you know? He should have let you—"

He held up a hand for a moment of silence. "Miss Kerwin. Hester. I am having a rather difficult time relating to this conversation. Would you mind coming down to my level just for a moment?"

"Oh, you'd like that, wouldn't you?" she sneered, or her knee sneered. "You'd like me to get practically down on the floor with you, wouldn't you? Patty-cake and hide-and-seek with the housekeeper, make the beds, toss the sheets, tea and biscuits in the morning without even a thank you very much, was it good for you too. Hey, you don't fool me, I know your kind. Sort. Station. You'd like nothing more than to tear this suit from my body to see what lies beneath, so you can satisfy your royal lust with the lonely servant, toss her aside like so much dish water, and leave town on the next carriage." A finger suddenly shook angrily in his face, forcing him to lean back and crack his head against the fireplace wall. "It's a damn good thing I'm way ahead of you."

"Hester," he said flatly, ignoring the sharp pain blossoming through his skull, "sit down."

She didn't move.

"Now."

A stormy indignant defiance filled the room for a brief moment before she relented, pulled up a chair, and sat. Adjusted her skirt. Fussed with her hair. Remarked upon the closeness of the room and removed her suit jacket, which did nothing for her ruffles but miracles for her shoulders.

"Thank you." He smiled without humor. He sniffed. He scanned the flooring for more neon spiders. He considered tenting his fingers under his chin and staring at her contemplatively, then decided such a theatrical pose would be a little much, considering the circumstances and the fact that she still had her gun. He settled for the staring. Without the contemplation; just a touch of intimidation.

"Thank you. Now. I would like you to explain what that scumbag, shyster, bloodsucker obviously didn't." He blinked. "Jesus, now you've got me doing it." He rubbed his face with his palms. "Please, Hester, let's be candid with each other for a change. Tell me what I'm obviously not meant to know until it's too late for me to do anything about what I didn't know until you told me. Tell me, for example, that I'm probably going to die before dawn because Howie the prick has set me up for a remarkable beyond-the-grave assassination. Tell me that this . . . this house has been deliberately denuded for my arrival in order to provide the maximum discomfort for my declining hours. Tell me that I have but . . . oh, shall we say one life to live? and it's about to be canceled any minute now."

She grinned.

He glared. "What the bloody hell's so funny?"

"Nothing." The grin remained. "You're just not as dumb as I thought you were."

The glare remained. "Is that some sort of clever American compliment?"

The grin broadened ever so slightly, but not without a certain appealing skew. "Nope. I just didn't think that you knew what you know, that's all. If I had known you had known all that, or if I had known that you had known, or at least suspected, that I knew, I know I wouldn't have worried, or been concerned, or fretted, or stewed about it so much."

"Stewed," he repeated with an acute sense of spiraling inevitability, "about what?"

"Your dying." Her shrug was alarmingly expressive: *Of course. What else?*

The glare was instantly replaced by a harsh barking laugh and a hearty slap to his knee.

"Hester, I assure you I am not planning to die."

Her grin was replaced by a knowing giggle. "I know that. It's Maclemmon's doing all the planning."

"He wants to kill me?"

She nodded.

This, he thought, goes beyond the realm of mere bilking from beyond the grave. It might even be serious.

"But he's dead," he pointed out.

She nodded.

"But somehow he's going to do it anyway."

She nodded.

"An assassin."

A shrug that told him he was close but don't light the cigar because he didn't have it yet and would probably only burn the hell out of his finger.

"When?"

"After the party."

"Ah."

"The shyster didn't tell you."

"No," he said. "He most certainly did not." He leaned forward, hands clasped. "You tell me."

"I—"

"Please."

She did.

He hated it.

"I hate it," he told her in no uncertain terms, although he couldn't help feeling that Howie's conniving grasp had finally exceeded his available reach, unless someone hadn't nailed the coffin lid down. "I don't mind telling you, a perfect stranger, that I hate it a lot."

"So would I if I were in your shoes. Thank God for small favors."

He put a thoughtful finger to the side of his nose, his jaw, his temple, his ear, his nose again. "So . . . unless there's a trick involved, like one of those deals with the Devil things where I turn the tables mere seconds from the potentially explosive finale, I'm either going to be torn to shreds a seamstress would weep over, or I leave in cowardly retreat and forfeit my inheritance. Is that about right?"

She nodded.

"And the rather tense scene in the restaurant a while ago. The gun and the demands part, I mean, not the waitress who tried to marry you off to someone she'd never met before in her busybody life. Nor am I referring to the gentlemen who stared at us so intently and left in such a hurry. That, the gun and the demands part, was your desperate and nearly effective way of attempting to keep me alive even though you knew that not staying here meant the total forfeiture of my legal inheritance and the death, so to speak, of my dreams."

She fluffed the ruffles, and nodded.

"I see."

"Didn't work, though."

"I see."

"So, you want to leave now?"

He thought a little, considered his options, weighed his choices, balanced the scales, flipped a coin.

"Tell me again," he requested. "Slowly. Without the thesaurus. Perhaps, together, we can figure out how to get around it."

"Why?"

"Well, damnit," he said, nearly yelling, "because I have only one life to live, in case you didn't catch that the first time, and I'd like to live it until I die in a more reasonable manner, thank you very much."

She told him.

He still hated it.

✦2✦

The plot thus far, according to Hester Kerwin, who should know:

Howmaster Maclemmon, after his last ignominious defeat at the vengeful hands of his lordship Kent Montana all those years ago, fled without delay to Europe since that was the direction in which he had been facing anyway. He traveled mostly on his wits because his shoes had been ruined during the Channel crossing, until, one dark and fairly turbulent evening, he reached a certain unnamed desolate valley in the interior of Luxembourg where, in the process of trying to con a wealthy but isolated medieval monastery into handing over its entire fortune on behalf of a lonely children's charity in South Liverpool, he discovered that the monastery's massive fortune wasn't worth nearly as much as its library was.

Books of such antiquity and rarity that he realized he could retire with the sale of just one of them until he needed money again.

But soon enough he realized that he didn't want just one of them.

He wanted the *Bingomomicron.*

He, like so many other scholars of ancient tomes written in ancient languages by dead people who weren't necessarily alive at the time of the writing, had never believed in its actual existence before; he had always derisively dismissed the rumors of that existence with a skeptical arrogant laugh; he had acidly scorned those who had claimed to have read it because, quite simply, it didn't exist.

Until now.

It was there; he had seen it. Locked solidly away in a centuries-old cabinet, behind a thick glass door blessed by generations of abbots whose sole duty, other than keeping the other monks in line, was to bless the glass and make sure it was never streaked after cleaning.

It was there.

He had seen it with his own eyes.

Bound it was in the supple tanned skin of excommunicated Mediterranean beach priests, written in the untainted blood of chastised nuns who didn't mind it all that much, scaled by yellowed wax formed from the inner thigh bones of a Hungarian saint martyred by being sealed into the foundation of a specialty butcher shop in Prague, papered by patterned parchment pressed from the reeds of a defunct Austrian orchestra, and painstakingly transcribed from the original indecipherable language with a pen fashioned from the thumbnails of a devil-worshipper nobody ever heard of because he either got it right, or lost his shirt, which was displayed, Howmaster noticed, in the next cabinet over.

The book was disgusting, obscene, and so insanely fanciful in its cosmic concepts as to make one wonder if it was not simply the fiction of a mind gone so far round the bend it had almost caught up with itself again at the next corner.

It was beautiful.

It was, as Maclemmon read haltingly by candlelight after all the other monks had gone sleepily to their cells, proof positive, or pretty sure, of a powerful race of Older Deities who had once ruled the Earth millennia ago and who, for reasons unknown because they weren't around anymore to explain it, had abandoned their advanced civilization and had returned to their ancient home among the stars.

It was a prophecy of their return.

It was a guarantee that Earth, as the monks and their children knew it, would never be the same again, especially since most everyone would be dead and those who remained would be rich as hell and twice as nasty.

It was, in Howmaster Maclemmon's feverish eyes, the key to paradise.

It was, in his increasingly demented and totally skewed mind, the perfect way to have his cake and eat it with Kent as the icing and those sweet little rose things around the edges.

Each chapter, he learned to his increasing delight, was a step in a series of esoteric rites that would guide the Older Deities from beyond the moon-bog nebula to the one spot on Earth where they would be able to land safely, without the hassle of discovery until they were good and ready to be discovered.

Each chapter he studied assiduously as he forced himself beyond the wall of sleep; each verse of each incomprehensible poem he memorized whether he understood it or not; each line of instruction he committed to heart, even though some of it made him a little queasy now and then.

And then, when he calculated the position of the stars and the moon and the line-up of the planets and realized that the Older Deities were in dire need of his assistance now and not several years hence by which time he would have finished his analysis, he panicked. It was over. He had come to this knowledge much too late. He was lost. Then, miraculously over a cup of corn tea he had cobbled together the next morning, he calmed, pondered, mused, and reflected, before doing the only sensible thing a complete nutter in his place would do under the circumstances.

He stole it.

To this very day, no one knows how, but in some mysterious and unscrupulous way he managed to conceal the bulky tome beneath his robes—for he had indeed become a member of the order in order to order the other monks around and give him unlimited access to the library—and sneak away during a night ominous with wild storms and rain and wind and hail and all sorts of dark flying things that kept the general population confined to their homes so they couldn't see him sneaking away.

Eventually he made his way to Rhode Island.

Eventually he purchased a pair of properties on Langford Place.

Eventually he gathered to his side a bunch of dedicated acolytes who were lured by the promise of everlasting life and lots of money.

Eventually he launched into the various varying rituals and ceremonies that would, if done properly, guide the Older Deities to Langford Place where they, the dedicated acolytes, would prostrate themselves before them, the Older Deities, and generally make them, the Older Deities, feel welcome before they, the Older Deities, smashed almost everything to a pulp. Except the dedicated acolytes.

The incredible psychic emanations from these rites and Saturday night meetings were evidently responsible for the civic decline of Hamtucket; the occasional foray into sacrificial victim gathering was clearly responsible for the declining population, less those who had moved away because of the rites and meetings which had devastated the town's economy; and the abrupt increase in natural disasters such as earthquakes and hurricanes could only be explained by the trans-universal vibrations created when the Older Deities responded with enthusiasm to the call of their new high priest.

Star paths had been charted.

Planetary orbits had been corrected and noted.

Calendars had been developed, discarded, redeveloped, burned, further explored in initial development, tested and revamped and tested again.

Finally the work was done.

At the annual summer solstice meeting and fried chicken barbecue behind John Laste's house, Maclemmon announced the time and date the Older Deities would arrive. And he also figured he knew, within six inches or so, where they would land.

The dedicated acolytes trembled with excitement.

However, Maclemmon in his madness explained that they needed one more victim. One more innocent lamb to the slaughter. One more sign so that the Older Deities would know that he truly was their earthly high priest on Earth, and that it was he who had shown them the way to the True Path of Landing, assuming there were no clouds. No rain date had been set.

Then, horribly, at least to the dedicated bunch of acolytes, Maclemmon was found dead in the middle of the street, his hair turned white, his skin blackened as if burned by a thousand matches or a blowtorch, and his lips parted in what one acolyte whose dedication had become a little shaky lately insisted was an incantation which proved that Maclemmon had been about to betray them all and bring the Older Deities in much earlier than was fashionable for this sort of thing.

A hasty convocation of the faithful decided, however, that they might as well go on with it since they couldn't stop it anyway, and as long as there was an heir to the estate, the heir might as well be the final sacrifice.

Kent Montana was to be the offering.

His blood was to fill the Sacred Soup Bowl of the Older Deities just in case they were thirsty from their long journey out of space.

His bones would be their meal.

His thighs would be their sofas.

His heart would be their snack.

His lungs would be the bellows to keep their interstellar fire aflame.

And when that was all over and the Older Deities sated, they would kill him.

And once he was dead, things he had not been meant to know would come to pass without his knowledge because he was, in the final analysis, dead.

Thus spaketh Hester Kerwin, who ought to know because it was she, and she alone, who had been Howmaster Maclemmon's lover, confidante, and Keeper of the *Bingomomicron* whenever Maclemmon didn't have it, which was hardly ever.

In point of fact, she had only had it once.

It had been enough.

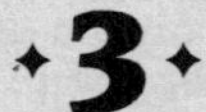

Kent Montana stood up, bowed to the astonished housekeeper, and marched purposefully to the front door without looking back. He was no fool most of the time; he knew full well that if he left the grounds, he would forfeit everything. He also knew full well that if he stayed in this unsavory manse, he would also forfeit everything because he'd be dead and therefore in no condition to complain. About anything. Weighing the death of a lifelong dream against the death of a long life proved, in the short run, to be no contest, mixed metaphorically speaking.

He opened the door.

"Be . . . ware," said the Russian peasant, clinging to his ironing board on the front porch.

Kent looked down at him from both height and station. "You're nuts."

"The indigenous crow flies backward this night," the little man continued, undeterred, and unconcerned that his cloth cap was rippling. "If you see him, you will die."

Hester hastened into the hall and gasped when she saw the Russian lurking so openly on the threshold.

Kent maintained his composure. "Crows are black."

The Russian blinked stupidly.

"Even if they were flying backward at night, I wouldn't be able to see them."

"Him," the Russian lurker on the threshold corrected with an upraised finger, although, technically speaking, he wasn't lurking anymore since everyone could see him and he wasn't trying to hide. Or lurk. Just forewarn. "Him. There's only one."

"Well, him is black, I wouldn't be able to see him, and besides, crows don't fly at night."

"Ah." The Russian cocked his head as if listening to the ironing board. "I . . . see."

Kent smiled patiently.

The Russian smiled back with what few teeth he had left, and those were black as crows, tipped his cap, and backed down the steps to the sidewalk.

Kent closed the door.

Hester peered through the triangular leaded glass pane beside the door. "He told me yesterday the flamingos were running back to Capistrano. I told him they were sparrows, and he said he didn't know sparrows were pink." She shook her head at the complexities of Man, then glared at him. "Hey, man, you were going to leave."

"Only in that I am going to live," he explained.

"Well, listen here, harken, and pay attention, Mr. Know-It-All Baron from a foreign country," she snapped indignantly. "You can leave, or you can stay, or you can dither here all night, it doesn't make any difference. The Older Deities are coming, and you can't run far enough to avoid them."

"Houston," he said.

She frowned, then scowled. "Is that some kind of upper class British humor thing?"

Guess not, he thought.

And I suppose, he continued as long as he was thinking and there wasn't much else going on at the moment, that if I do leave, all of this will be damned inconvenient for my conscience. Assuming the world is around long enough to let me have a conscience. The question, among others, is: Can I live with it? Can I face myself cheerfully each sunny morning without screaming, knowing that the utter destruction of half the civilized world, and France, is all my fault because I did nothing to prevent it? Can I film a film for all to enjoy when all to enjoy aren't? Can I afford to let all those people die when they could be buying tickets instead?

What kind of a man are you, Kent Montana, which isn't your real name but who the hell cares, if you're going to die at dawn?

What sort of son did your mother raise, other than an extremely cautious one?

What kind of supposedly sensitive human being are you that you would allow other human beings to die horrible, terrible, gory, and undoubtedly disgusting deaths at the hands, or whatever, of prehistorically deified creatures from outer space who used to rule this world and want another shot at it?

And what, exactly, lurks behind all those pale yellow ruffles?

Hester tapped his chest with a forefinger.

He shook his head quickly. "Huh?"

"If you ask yourself any more questions," she told him sympathetically, "you'll faint."

He laughed. "I have a tendency," he confessed.

"I noticed."

As if a great weight had been lifted from his shoulders and dropped on his head, he clapped his hands once, rubbed his palms together briskly, and said, "All right, Miss Kerwin, all right, you win. Lead me to the *Bingomomicron* without delay. We'll do our duty and let Howmaster know he didn't have the last word after all."

She threw her arms around him.

He embraced her.

She kissed him gratefully.

He kissed her back, gratefully but not the same, and slightly puzzled because her lips, while they were very nice lips indeed, were also somewhat familiar lips beyond the fact that they were, unquestionably, real lips.

However, before he could kiss her again just to check the validity of his perceptions, she pulled away reluctantly, glanced through the hall window again, and said, "But what about John and Marsha and Caroline and Rex and Wally and Quentin and Ivan and Pilandra, and maybe even Sheila?"

"Rex?"

She checked her wristwatch. "Damn, it's already long after eight. They'll be here in two hours, more or less." Panic flitted across her eyes and made her blink. "My god, so much to do, so little time."

He smiled and took her arms gently to calm her. "It's all right, Miss Kerwin. Don't worry about it. We'll just have a surprise for them, that's all." A thoughtful, perilously close to decisive, nod. "But first we must dress for this sham occasion. We cannot, of course, let them know that we know that what they know isn't true, because we know something they don't know." A wink. "I don't suppose there's any food?"

"I was going to order out."

"Ah." He reached down to pick up his suitcase, and realized with a start that it wasn't there. Not only wasn't it there, it wasn't even in the house because he'd left it back at the Gutted Oyster. "Damn."

Someone knocked on the door.

They exchanged nervous glances.

The knocking grew louder.

Kent took a deep breath, tucked it into his lungs, and answered the summons.

"Actually," said the little Russian, handing over Kent's suitcase with his free hand, "it was more sideways like."

Kent closed the door.

One of those nights, he figured; it was going to be, aside from the sacrifice and the Older Deities, one of those goddamn nights.

Hester, seeing that he teetered dangerously on the verge of thinking again, snatched the suitcase from his grip, picked up the flashlight on the first step of the staircase, and said without a trace of shame, "Walk this way."

Kent glanced at the ceiling, pleading fervently for strength, courage, and a little taste for a change. Then he followed her to the second floor which was, essentially, a large, long rectangular hall off of which, in the center of each wall, was a room. She brought him to the back room, put down his suitcase, handed him the flashlight, told him not to be too long, and vanished into the dark.

Kent wasted no time theorizing or ruminating, much less looking for a place to hang his clothes. If he was to get out of here alive, and with Stellar Artists Productions in his pocket, he had to assume the mantle of a man of action. It damn near choked him, but he managed to get it on anyway, then flipped open the suitcase, untied the silken ties that held his suits and trousers and shirts and socks and underwear snugly into place, stripped, shivered, and proceeded, in time-honored baronial fashion, to pull his jeans on one leg at a time. He had tried the other way once and had nearly broken his back. Then he put his shirt on one sleeve at a time, socks one foot at a time, sturdy western boots in the usual manner, which meant a lot of hopping about on one foot and slamming into the walls, and finally, a bulky tartan cardigan which would serve not only to guard against the fact that the house had no heat to speak of, and so he said nothing, but also to provide him with a conveniently deep pocket for the especially manufactured Aberdeen revolver he took from a secret compartment in his suitcase lid.

One never knew, when one was going face to whatever with the Older Deities, when one would need something to shoot them with.

And if they didn't show up, there was always that damned Russian.

As soon as he was finished, he retied the ties, closed the suitcase, stuck it in a corner so no one would trip over it, and stepped into the hall.

Aside from the usual creaking and settling of old, tired wood, the house was silent.

Except, unfortunately, for the wind. It was pretty loud, screaming and howling in the eaves the way it was, rattling the windows and doors, and puffing down the chimney.

Other than that, however, it was silent.

Caution, and a carefree sense of in for a penny, what the hell, led him reluctantly to explore the other rooms, which were empty, dusty, and dark.

Then, suddenly and without warning, he noticed a fifth door.

He squinted at it, looked up, and realized it must lead to the attic.

Did he, he wondered, want to go up there?

Was such a thorough investigation of the house's inner reaches absolutely, positively, unquestionably necessary in order to assure his and Hester's safety during the coming trials and tribulations?

"Hey!" Hester called from the bottom of the stairs. "In case you didn't know, there's a—"

"Don't bother," he told her sourly, and opened the door.

Meanwhile . . .

John Laste opened the bedroom closet, pressed a small button just to the right of the frame, and pushed through the two hundred tailored suits arranged in pinstripe order into a secret room at the back. There he examined the assembled arsenal on the wall. His private collection. It had cost him hundreds of thousands of dollars over the years, but the comfort the weapons gave him just in the knowing they were here was well worth it, except for the tax when he purchased them legitimately and wrote them off as a business expense.

He would need something tonight.

Not as protection against the others, because they were weak and venal and disgusting little creatures who would be taken care of in due course.

No.

He needed something to use against Kent Montana.

It took him fifteen minutes before he settled on the perfect instrument.

After examining it closely to be sure its components were in working order, he tucked it neatly into his inside evening jacket pocket, especially made to conceal such a weapon. Then he turned off the light, pushed back through the suits, pressed the button, and stepped into the bedroom.

"Darling," Marsha said, stepping out of her clothes closet and fussing with her lace and silk bodice because the emerald one had been too cold, "were you in the weapons room again?"

Sweat trickled down his spine.

"Honestly." She bent over her vanity, patted her hair, smudged out a wrinkle, and started for the hall. "You men are just like little boys, aren't you? Always playing with things that can hurt you."

He stared after her.

There was a cautionary signal in that seemingly innocuous statement. He knew it. And he knew that it must have something to do with his clandestine affair with Caroline Putney. Unless, he thought as he hurried after her, it had something to do with his secret financial dealings with kindly Kenilworth Smith. Of course, it may have nothing at all to do with any of it. It may just be a simple, potent warning that she knew all about his brief furtive dalliance with that dumbass actor kid's mother, and she was ready to forgive him.

Or, he thought as he stumbled down the stairs where Marsha was already waiting with their pre-dinner and sacrifice cocktail, it was a threat.

Damn, he thought as he marveled aloud at his wife's beauty and taste, women can be so sneaky sometimes.

Meanwhile . . .

Wally Putney adjusted his clip-on club tie so that it cleverly concealed the Velcro strip that held his nylon tight-mesh shirt together. Then he slipped into his Oxford loafers, fluffed the tassels, checked himself in the mirror, and decided that he was about as ready as he'd ever be.

He was nervous.

So much was at stake tonight, so many disparate yet common futures riding on the back of one man, that he hoped they wouldn't serve anything really greasy, or he'd probably embarrass himself.

No. Never mind. Nothing embarrassed him anymore. Nothing had since those nightmarish years in grade school, where he had first gotten used to the unthinking cruelty of others as they teased him about his weight, his myopia, his intelligence, his mother, his father, his four brothers and three sisters, his fortune, his dog, his parakeet, his stubbed nose, his knocked knees, his shoes, his airplane, his limpid hair, and his stutter. He had outgrown most of it now, except for the stubbed nose and the limpid hair, but he was still crushed by the weight of a complex so complex that complexity was a mere word in the words that described his complex psychological affliction.

He went downstairs.

He stepped into the living room just as Caroline switched off the television and swirled around to greet him.

He sighed with both delight and melancholy. She was so beautiful, so ethereal, so seductive and yet so innocent in her pink chiffon gown and black velvet choker with the diamond in the middle. At that moment there wasn't anything he wouldn't do for her. Too bad she was a slut.

"Wally!" she said delightedly.

He preened at her blatant adoration. "Caroline, darling, we're going to be late if we don't hurry. We still have our evening perambulation to do. Stimulating the appetite, remember? Good for the juices."

She pouted. "Wally."

He smiled benevolently and checked the kitchen to be sure Puffball had enough to eat, checked the locks on all the doors and windows, and checked to be sure he had the weapon safely tucked into his trouser pocket. Caroline hadn't mentioned it all evening, but he knew she was aware that he had it. It was he, after all, who had volunteered to do the necessary deed since he couldn't bear the thought of trying to get all that blood out of all that chiffon. She had, fortunately, seen the wisdom of it, especially when he had demonstrated how proficient he was with the instrument.

"Wally!" she had gasped.

God, it felt good!

"Wally?" she chided now, pointing to the emerald watch on her wrist.

"All right, dear," he said. He fetched their coats, helped her into his, and opened the front door.

The fog had thickened.

The wind blew like a son of a bitch.

And Wally Putney smiled smugly to himself.

"You know, Caroline," he said as they stepped into the brisk October night, "I almost feel sorry for that Kent Montana." He chuckled and hugged her arm to his side. "Almost. But not quite."

"Oh . . . Rex," she breathed.

"Rex?"

"Wally!"

"I'm sorry, darling. It's the fog. Messes up my ears."

But she didn't see the look that crossed his face.

And he didn't see the first step.

"Wally!" she scolded after he had hit the bottom.

And Wally Putney, for the first time in his life, almost glared.

Meanwhile . . .

Dr. Kenilworth Smith paced his cluttered living room apprehensively and not very carefully. Tables had been knocked askew, a chair had toppled, and his bottle of bourbon, empty though it was, had broken on the hearth.

The problem, however, was not the room's disarray; it was his black bag.

He didn't know if he should bring it or not.

While there was bound to be a lot of blood and abrasions and lacerations and contusions and missing limbs, if he walked into Number 668 with the tell-tale bag in hand, Kent Montana might suspect something. And if he suspected something, something might go wrong. And if something went wrong, it might all go wrong and what the hell would they do then, the Older Deities coming and all.

He cleared his throat; he scratched his cheek; he paced once more and knocked over the grandfather clock his grandfather had brought over from the Old Country. The subsequent bedlam of dented chimes and sprung springs forced him to a decision:

He would bring the bag.

If anyone was to be so gauche as to ask, he could say that he had brought it with him to Omaha and hadn't had a chance to drop it off at the house before coming over. Although Caroline would certainly see through the ruse instantly, he knew he could deal with her later. It was Montana he was concerned about.

Maybe he should leave it; it might be more trouble than it was worth.

He scowled at the darkened room, scowled at his vacillating indecision, and finally, decisively, stomped into his office and grabbed the bag.

The hell with it.

If they made a fuss, he would expose them all and be damned to them. Except for Rex. He had no idea who the hell Rex was, but he had the distinct feeling that exposing Rex wouldn't be such a good idea. He didn't know why; he called it physician's instinct, and save for the time when he had treated Pilandra Eddye for that persistent chest cold last summer in Hawaii, his instinct was never wrong.

A few adjustments were made to the bag's contents, and ten minutes later he stood at attention at the living room window, watched the pre-Halloween wind tousle the last of the dead leaves in the trees, watched the fog drift languidly up and down the street, and hefted the bag in both hands, just to be sure he could feel the reassuring weight of the weapon hiding under all those drugs.

He smiled.

A little dog howled.

Well, Mr. Montana whoever you are, he thought gleefully, it's time to get you up on the old examination table and see what you're made of.

"Heh," he chuckled evilly to the empty room. "Heh. Heh. Heh."

Rex Regal, as he was known to the inhabitants of Langford Place, hid in the shadows under an oak tree at the north end of the street. His tuxedo was so perfectly tailored that it was impossible to see the change when he pulled the eye patch from his pocket and settled it over his left eye; nor did the tuxedo betray the weapon he carried in his inside, left breast pocket.

From his hip pocket he pulled a jeweled compact and, using the streetlamp for light, checked his disguise.

He nodded satisfaction.

He straightened his spine.

He took the first step down the street and smiled when he realized that momentous journeys such as this always begin with the first step, that tonight was the first night of the first day of the rest of his life, that all things come to he who waits.

That Kent Montana was a dead man and didn't know it.

His laugh was short and sharp.

Simultaneously . . .

"Rex?" said Kent Montana, halfway up the attic steps.

Meanwhile . . .

"Son," said Pilandra Eddye as she escorted her son to the door, "I'm very proud of you."

"Mom, I still feel like a jerk."

She winked playfully. "But you're a cute jerk, you jerk. Now get out there and . . . knock 'em dead."

He kissed her cheek.

She kissed his cheek and pushed him playfully out the door.

She waved until the fog and wind swallowed him.

She closed the door and leaned against it.

"Bog-Muggoth," she said, "you screw me around this time, I'll have your spacial balls."

Then she hastened into the kitchen where she was boiling water so that she could, if called upon, deliver Sheila Verlin's illegitimate baby; unless it was Caroline's. All these years, she'd never been able to keep them straight.

Except, of course, for Rex.

She giggled.

She sighed her relief. At least he wouldn't be a party to the party that night.

She froze.

My god, suppose he was there. Never in his life had he been able to pass up a party.

My god, suppose he saw . . . Quentin!

My god.

Sheila Verlin, who had just turned twenty a few months ago, stood forlornly at the front window of her struggling home and watched through the intermittent gaps in the fog and the wind as the primary elite of Langford Place prepared to gather for entrance into Number 668.

When she spotted Quentin in his breath-taking seersucker Sunday best crossing the street, waving cheerily to kindly Dr. Smith, who was standing on his porch and ugly enough to keep the fog and wind at bay and prevent her darling Quentin from tripping into the gutters, her impressionable heart leapt high and she choked with suppressed emotion. Then her pulse raced until she caught up with it and whirled to the others strewn pathetically about the room.

"I don't care," she announced defiantly, her delicate hands fisted petitely at her sides. "You can take care of yourselves for one night, do you hear me? This night is mine! This is my life! This is my song of independence. This," she declared, "is where I get off!"

"Darling?" her long-suffering father croaked from his seven-position hospital bed in front of the large-screen television. "Would you mind changing my oxygen tank first?"

"Sweetheart?" gasped her mother from her motorized wheelchair beside the hospital bed in front of the large-screen television set. "Would you please fetch my I'll-have-a-heart-attack-and-die-if-I-don't-take-them pills before you go?"

Her sister waddled pregnantly into the room. "I think it's time."

Her brother withdrew into a corner of his cage and whimpered about the sky falling and wasn't anybody paying attention to his needs for a change?

Sheila stared angrily at them all. If she left, they would be helpless; if she stayed, she would miss out meeting this mysterious Montana Quentin spoke so often about; if she left, they might all perish or get in pretty bad shape; if she stayed, she'd miss out messing around with Quentin's seersucker; if she left; if she stayed.

She whirled back to the window and watched a sleek taxi pull up in front of Number 697 to wait for the Lastes. Oh Lord, she thought, won't you buy me a Mercedes-Benz and get me the hell out of here?

"Darling?"

"Sweetheart?"

"Sister?"

"Whimper."

God, she thought irreverently, I hate being a saint.

Later, but not by much . . .

The marble winged woman flexed her wings again and dropped the vase.

"Damn," she said.

The water boiled in the marble bowl.

- IV -

Another World

Out in space, where no one can hear you scream because if they were in a position to do so they'd be just as dead as you were about to be even before you had a chance to scream, something awfully sinister and large and suspicious *moved* around the misty edges of the Crab Nebula, just two and a half parsecs from the spiraling fringe of the Moon-Bog Nebula. It might have been mites, but reputable astronomers doubted it. Rather, it seemed to be *movement* of a kind none of them had ever observed before, in space.

It appeared to be a great, spreading, thick, lightless, undulating black cloud.

Or one hell of a large malleable spaceship.

Within minutes of the first verifiable sightings, telephones began ringing frantically in various civilian and military offices around the world; cautionary telegrams were sent between heads of state; excited conversations exploded excitedly in executive cafeterias and hallways, private parking lots and public bars; infrared, photospectronic, stop-motion, and space photographs were taken and developed, hasty sketches were made in trembling freehand, and boring verbal descriptions were recorded for oral history.

That this black . . . thing . . . seemed to be heading for Earth was not debatable; what it would do when it got here, on the other hand, was something none of the astronomers wanted to consider. That was something for their bosses, their governments, and their cheap-labor graduate assistants to worry about. All they, the astronomers, wanted was an opportunity for a little pure science just to liven things up.

It never occurred to any of them that the steadily increasing numbers of people chanting and wailing and prostrating and humbling and flagellating themselves in the streets and alleys and strip malls of every major capital in the world except Paris were more right than they would ever know. At least the prostrated ones were—they wouldn't have to fall down when they were squashed by the undulating shadow out of space.

Stars began to vanish as the black . . . thing . . . approached.

Ambient light waves refracted back upon themselves for a second look.

Sound waves were muffled.

One Siberian scientist, visiting the exotic hinterlands of Washington State with his zaftig teenage niece, suggested rather timidly to his skeptical colleagues that the black . . . thing . . . seemed almost . . . alive.

Another scientist in Edinburgh suggested the same thing to his wife.

Still another, in Athens, was so bold as to proclaim it.

Nobody, however, took them seriously.

Too bad.

– V –

The Romance of Helen Trent

She met this guy who looked pretty much like Rex Regal, except that it wasn't, fell in love, had lots of troubles, solved most of them and ignored the others, had lots of children who gave her lots of joy and more troubles, and a whole passel of grandchildren.

Then she died.

The end.

– VI –

The Gathering Storm

✦1✦

Kent was not enamored of attics, nor did he like them very much. In his experience, not counting the time his nanny had locked him in one with a ravenous boar, they were usually filled with lots of musty dead clothes hanging in cracked plastic cocoons from hooks pounded into rafters, dead steamer trunks filled with dead clothes smelling like stale lavender and moldy bread, dead cardboard boxes and orange crates filled with dead artifacts of forgotten childhoods and previous marriages, piles of dead magazines and newspapers and letters, and lots of invisible things that weren't dead crawling around among all the dead things. There was also dust and cobwebs and the dried husks of invisible things that finally died among all the dead things.

Thus, when his flashlight beam swept boldly through the attic of Number 668, he allowed himself a modicum of suspicious surprise when he perceived that there was nothing in the attic that looked even remotely dead, musty, or rotting, except for the mummy case. In fact, except for the mummy case, there wasn't anything in the attic at all.

He frowned.

Curious.

Nevertheless, he made a guarded but thorough circumnavigation of the huge, almost empty room just in case some dead things of significance were lurking in the corners which, he noted with another modicum of mild surprise, there weren't any of since the attic was round even though the outside of the attic, including the roof, wasn't.

He frowned.

Curious.

He wondered what Hester would make of this apparent anomaly in New England housing construction, and decided that he didn't want to know. It was enough that she believed that he believed in all this blather about Older Deities, sacrifices, the end of the world, and Howmaster Maclemmon being the cause of it all. Howie the prick had been the cause of a lot of things during his dubious lifetime, but precipitating the end of the world by outer space gods arriving in gold chariots made in Peru wasn't one of them. It was, he was still positive, all part and parcel of the man's plan.

The uncomfortable house, the outlandish story, the housekeeper, the spooky neighborhood—Maclemmon had obviously arranged every bit of it from the start, and had he not died so suddenly and so mysteriously and so weirdly, no doubt there would be even more.

He grinned.

Not bad, actually, Howie old son, he thought in memorial commemoration even though the man had been a thoroughgoing bastard; the organ's a bit much though.

Of course, when he thought about it, there was the mysterious and weird death.

"Stop," he muttered as he completed his prowling.

Howmaster, for all his faults, had always kept himself in excellent condition.

"Stop."

And why, if this was all part of the wee bastard's final elaborate scam and probable bilking, did his hair turn white overnight?

"Enough."

What in fact had Howie inadvertently or otherwise set in motion that had so unnerved him that he had run screaming into the middle of the street in the middle of the night and dropped rather dead?

Kent, he scolded sternly, belt up. You're playing right into his hands, don't you see that? confusing yourself with a lot of heavy thinking, a lot of penetrating questions, and a lot of loose and flashy speculation, when the answers are clear as the nose on your face.

The flashlight went out.

He yelped, banged it frantically against the wall, and sagged in relief when the beam once again soared weakly across the spacious room, this time highlighting a long knotted cord hanging from a rusty hook embedded in a ceiling beam. Closer inspection proved it to be a cord filled with knots, and he realized that if he should be stupid enough to pull on it, it would release a spring-ladder which would, if he were dumb enough to climb it, take him to the roof where, no doubt, Howmaster had his telescope bolted, and probably a trap rigged to blow Kent into the next town.

Curious.

He headed back to the stairs.

Say there, m'lord, a part of him that obviously didn't belong in a situation like this asked, aren't you going to check that mummy case over there?

He paused.

It was, all things considered, a fair question, and one any reasonable human being would ask if they too were stupid enough to be up here.

However, in equal fairness to his lordship, there were a lot of curious things up here, and he definitely wasn't one of them. The mummy case was indeed arresting in an exotic, deathlike sort of morbid way, but it wasn't encased in sparkling rare jewels or banded in glittering Nile gold or etched in reflective Memphis silver or marked with an ancient Cairo curse written in cryptic hieroglyphics at the base. As a matter of fact, it had Howmaster's pudgy face painted on top and the ensuing replica of his equally pudgy body was surrounded by all the usual Egyptian-looking things mummy cases had on them, and there was no way in hell he was going to open it.

Then it occurred to him that while the attorney had made some passing mention of Maclemmon's funeral, a simple affair with only a handful of paid mourners, he hadn't actually said that Howie had been buried. At least not in a cemetery. At least not in the ground.

He looked at the mummy case.

The mummy case looked back.

"No," he whispered. "Too obvious."

So open it.

The doorbell gonged.

Instincts in both a butler and self-preservation sense instantly swept over him, and without a backward glance at the mummy case, or the knotted cord, he hurried down to the first floor, dusted the attic's dusty residue from his clothes as best he could, and opened the door.

"My god!" gasped an extraordinarily blond young man as he stumbled back a step at Kent's appearance. "My god, I don't believe it, it's really you!"

Kent waited for the Russian to show up, unless this young man was the Russian with a shave and a seersucker suit that was, at best, a size too large. Then, as the young man attempted to compose himself, he squinted as something tingled at the back of his mind still up there with the mummy case.

"I know you, don't I?" he said at last.

"I'm dead," the young man answered.

There is a lesson here, Kent thought, that I am doomed not to learn.

The young man blushed handsomely in a manly sort of way, and shoved a nervous hand through his shaggy hair. "That is, I was dead when I saw you. Or you saw me. But I didn't know you saw me, see. I was dead, see, and you . . ." He laughed. "That doesn't make much sense, does it?"

Suddenly Kent smiled broadly. "A-hah! Of course! Yes! You . . . don't tell me now, I'll get it, I'm rather good at this sort of thing . . . you were the cousin murdered by Vanessa's twin sister, Janine, who pinned the crime on Vanessa so that she wouldn't marry Herbert, even though Herbert was already married to Lillian, who secretly loved you but was going to marry Herbert so that she could divorce Steve and have your child instead of Steve's or Herbert's, even though both Steve and Herbert would think the child was theirs."

"Lord," said Quentin Eddye, awe settling handsomely over his features.

"Baron will do nicely," Kent told him kindly, and shook his hand. "So what have you been doing since you died?"

A woman screamed.

Without thinking, Kent leapt onto the porch, Quentin leapt onto the railing, and they both looked down the street alertly.

I don't like this, Kent thought.

The woman screamed again.

Not a bit.

The scream was not fear-induced, however, nor was it one of extreme and enviable ecstasy.

It was one of violent, vicious, frustrated anger.

"We have to help her," Quentin said.

"I can't," said Kent.

"Butlers aren't allowed to help people?"

"I'm not a butler, I'm a baron, and I can't leave this house until dawn, the porch doesn't count."

"Hell, I know that, but aren't you going to help her anyway?"

"Who?"

Quentin pointed. "Her."

The air had cleared somewhat, even though it was still dark. The fog had lifted, leaving behind small cloudlike patches that hung in front of the houses across the street as if they had been painted there. Dead leaves and a rat stirred restlessly in the gutters. A dog barked. The organ tuned up. A cat howled. The streetlamps buzzed and dimmed, but not so much that Kent couldn't see the pale, draped, winged marble woman struggling on her hands and knees up the middle of the tarmac.

It was she who was screaming.

Just as Kent was about to ask a pertinent question, and dread the response, Hester leapt onto the porch, ruffles rippling. "I heard a scream."

The two men pointed.

Hester looked. "Jesus Christ, it's started, and the rolls aren't even done yet."

Quentin paled. "It's started?"

"What's started?" Kent asked.

"He said there would be harbingers," Hester told Quentin. "Don't you remember? He said there'd be like scouts or something."

The marble woman screamed.

Another woman screamed.

"My god!" Quentin cried. "It's Sheila!"

"Sheila?" Kent said.

"Sheila, darling, stay where you are!" Quentin yelled heroically, and leapt from the railing to the ratty lawn in a single athletic bound, tumbled to his knees, rolled over, scrambled to his feet, and ran to the left where, Kent saw, a young woman in designer jeans and a light sweater stood frozen with terror in the middle of the street.

He looked right—the winged marble woman crawled on, screaming with rage, her wings flapping stiffly, her hands tearing up the tarmac.

He looked left—Quentin had nearly reached the young woman, although a tree had gotten in the way there for a while.

He looked right—the marble woman with wings came inexorably on.

He looked left—Quentin reached the woman, whose name was obviously Sheila, scooped her up in his arms, and ran back toward the house.

He looked right—the marble woman had made oh, maybe ten feet.

Quentin raced up the stairs after tripping over the curb and set the young woman lightly on her feet. She saw Kent. She gasped. She curtsied. He nodded. She looked at Quentin, who said, "It's okay, Sheila, he's a regular joe. We knew each other when I was dead."

"Started," Hester whispered.

"What's started?" Kent asked.

Hester turned on him and slapped his shoulder, hard. "You! You let that poor boy go out there all by himself to rescue his lover? You let him face that . . . that creature, thing, abomination, monster on his own? What are you, some kind of pervert?"

He looked at the marble woman.

He looked at Hester. "I can't. You know that."

The organ chided.

The woman screamed; the marble one.

Hester was clearly appalled. "You mean to tell me you put your own greed, avarice, and cupidity ahead of the safety of these two young people?"

He reached for her arm.

She snatched it away.

He grabbed it and yanked her close, ignored her struggles although the ruffles were rather distracting, and pointed. "That woman, may I point out, is made of marble. Dakota, if I'm not mistaken. That woman has gone about fifteen feet in the time we've been out here. That woman can't fly because her wings are made of marble too. That woman won't be at the end of the block by noon."

Hester's mouth opened. Closed.

"Kent," Quentin suggested, "I don't think she's going to the end of the block."

Kent looked.

The boy was right.

The winged marble woman had veered from her previous course and was heading directly for the house. His house. The one he was standing outside of, which happenstance was, he sensed instantly, a mistake when she raised her head, saw him, and smiled nastily as best she could since her lips couldn't move except when she screamed.

She didn't scream.

Sheila did.

"It's started," Hester whispered. "Lord preserve us, it's started."

"What's started?" Kent demanded, sitting sidesaddle on the railing to watch the marble winged woman topple slowly to her side when one of her aesthetically lovely but aerodynamically lousy wings tried to flex and over-balanced her.

"The End."

"Ah."

Sheila screamed again, whimpered, flung herself into Quentin's arms and buried her face in his chest.

Hester slapped Kent's shoulder, hard. "You didn't believe me, did you, you forking bastard?" she said, hurt and astonished and angry and fairly close to humiliation. "You've never believed me, ever."

"I've only known you a couple of hours," he reminded her. "I cannot help but think never is a bit strong."

She hit him again, pretty good.

He looked at her.

She looked back, proud and defiant and daring him to sock her in the jaw.

His eyes widened.

"Say, Mr. Montana?" Quentin said, after disinterring Sheila from his chest.

Hester sneered.

Kent said, slowly, "Those tapes. In your purse. They're from an English language course, aren't they."

"Uh, Baron?"

Hester blanched as best she could with a name like Hester and gestured urgently to the marble woman with the wings, who was almost at the curb. "My god, we have to stop her, m'lord. She'll kill us all in our beds or wherever."

Kent grinned. "Miss, you certainly have a peculiar accent for one who lives in Rhode Island." Then he added, meaningfully, *"Hester."*

"Jesus, Baron!"

Hester's hands fluttered to her chest, ruffled the ruffles in pointless distraction, and pointed. "My god, we're all going to die!"

Kent laughed.

"Lord," said Quentin, "is he brave or what?"

Sheila partially swooned.

"Quentin," Kent said without taking his eyes from Hester's eyes, or the rest of her, "be a good lad and nip into the kitchen, would you? I'm sure there's a convenient drawer in one of the cabinets which holds certain common household tools. Fetch us a hammer and a couple of chisels, if you don't mind."

"Damn," Quentin said to Sheila, "why didn't I think of that?"

The young people rushed into the house.

Kent took his time standing to his full height.

Then, in a blurred and not easily seen motion, he reached out and snatched Hester's hair from her head.

"You," he said, not altogether disappointed.

"So," said the woman who was thought to be Hester Kerwin up until this point but obviously wasn't, "we gonna kick marble ass or what?"

•2•

A trio of elegantly dressed gentlemen stood at the mouth of Langford Place. Though they spoke not a word to each other, a passer-by would have understood at once that they were debating whether or not to stay where they were, move deeper into the street, or walk on past it.

The tallest, at the last, held the deciding vote, and he cast it in favor of moving on, so that they might return later, at a more propitious and dramatic time.

The short one pouted.

The middle-size one shrugged.

And they did walk on, silently and elegantly, although the tall one admittedly felt a certain twinge of apprehension about his decision since, if it was the wrong one, Kent Montana would be too dead to help when they returned.

But, he thought philosophically, the road of life is constantly filled with many obstacles to overcome, and as the world turns on its celestial axis, even the bold and the beautiful are ofttimes prone to error.

He sighed.

They walked on.

• • •

Dr. Kenilworth Smith was about to step off his porch and make his fateful journey across the street, when he heard the unmistakably melodic ring of his Swedish telephone in the office. He hesitated. He opened the door. He looked down the hall toward his office, where the telephone was. He wondered if it might be an emergency, requiring his expert medical or research services, or . . . something else.

The telephone rang.

The organ prodded.

Frowning, he checked his watch, saw that he would be too early for the food or the killing anyway, and hastened back inside, to the very room where so many of his medical and personal triumphs had been realized. He cleared his throat and picked up the receiver.

"Smith? Dr. Kenilworth Smith?"

"Yes."

"Do you know who this is?"

"Well, of course I don't, you fool. I just picked up the receiver. I do know who you sound like, but you can't be him because he's dead."

"Well, it is me, Dr. Smith, and I can assure you I wasn't dead the last time I looked."

The shock staggered Kenilworth into his plush leather chair. "But that's . . . it's . . . impossible!"

"Why, Doctor, are you saying that it's too late in the game for a new player?"

"Sir, I do not know what you are referring to."

The caller cackled and wheezed. "Oh, Doctor, your physician humor always was pretty sharp."

Kenilworth gasped. Sweat poured from his brow. "What . . . what do you want?"

"Why, Dr. Smith, you surprise me. I thought you would have already guessed by now, your physician's instinct being as accurate and infallible as it is—I . . . want . . . to . . . kill . . . you."

Smith slammed the receiver down with a trembling hand. It wasn't bad enough that the Older Deities were about to land and reward their dedicated bunch of servants; now he had to put up with some doddering sonofabitch who wanted revenge for a past sin which was, in the past, awfully bad but now, through the corrective lens of hindsight, wasn't all that terrible. Nobody had died, after all; there were lots of people with only one leg who were able to do all sorts of things nowadays. Why should this happen to him now? Why should he, a reasonably decent human being except for Caroline and a murky past, be slated for punishment now? Why?

He sat in the dark.

He trembled.

And when he finally managed to gain control, he pulled open a secret drawer of his teakwood desk and took out a gun. It was loaded. Very loaded. With a surgeon's steady hands, he dropped it into his black bag, below the stuff he was going to use to kill Kent Montana with. Then he stood, strode into the kitchen, used a towel to dry the sweat from his face and neck, and cleared his throat.

It was time.

Nobody, not even Lorenzo Jones, would keep him from his destiny.

By cracky.

Wally Putney had remained outdoors for a few moments longer after the pre-feast and sacrifice perambulation had ended, to breathe in the last of the fog as it lifted languidly from Langford Place. The short yet intimate walk through the park had been delightful, if somewhat one-sided conversation-wise, yet he needed a little time alone to gather his thoughts and figure out how things were going to go, later, when the world as he knew it ended and he was in charge.

Then he heard the telephone's distinctive ring, but thought nothing of it until he went inside and, although he didn't eavesdrop, he couldn't help note with a tiny prickling of alarm that his wife had wound a piece of the hallway's scarlet flocked wallpaper around her little finger and was tearing the hell out of it with her teeth.

He expressed his puzzlement nonverbally.

When Caroline finally hung up, pale and shaken, she stumbled blindly into the alabaster living room and leaned dramatically against the mantel over the place where the fireplace would have been if he'd remembered to put it in the building plans. "Oh, Wally," she said in evident despair.

His eyes widened. "What?" he demanded.

Her eyes, already wide, filled with glistening tears. "Oh . . . Wally."

At the sight, and the message, he came as close to gasping as he ever had in his life. As it was, he gulped. But it couldn't be. After all these years? After all that water under the bridge? After all the care he had taken? It couldn't be. Not tonight, of all nights.

He dropped heavily onto the sofa and clasped his hands between his knees. "Caroline, I don't know what to say."

"Wally."

"But how was I to know she was still alive . . . after? I thought we had . . . you know. I mean, we personally watched the car plummet off the bridge into the recently rain-flooded canyon." He looked at her and bit his lower lip until he tasted blood. "We saw the fire, the flames, the smoke, the steam." The lip quivered. "She couldn't have lived, Caroline. She just couldn't have."

Caroline, made of sterner stuff and pink chiffon, strode across the room and grabbed his shoulders. "Wally," she admonished.

He whimpered.

"Wally."

"You're right." He sat up straight. "You're absolutely right, my darling. Tonight, of all nights, we must become partners again, shoulder to shoulder, facing it all together, we'll never give up, we'll never give up because, my love, we are the favored favorite children of the Older Deities, and *we shall not fail.*"

"My, Wally," she breathed, impressed by his burst of manliness.

But Wally Putney wasn't thinking about impressing his slut of a wife; he was thinking about how he was going to have to enlist one of the Others, perhaps Kenilworth if he was sober, to get rid of his slut of an ex-wife before the Older Deities came and did the job for him.

This was something he had to do for himself For his self-esteem. For his pride. For his freedom.

Caroline tapped her sapphire watch.

He nodded. "All right, darling," he said.

Caroline smiled.

He kissed her lightly on the cheek.

She slapped him playfully on the rump and hurried off to the downstairs powder room to powder whatever.

When she was gone, Wally quickly checked his weapon. His expression was grim. And he hoped his undead ex-wife wouldn't mind that she wouldn't be around long enough to watch him kill Kent Montana.

• • •

The telephone rang.

John Laste, who had been watching a drunken woman in an outrageous Halloween costume crawl drunkenly up the street in time to the ridiculously accurate accompaniment of someone's electronic organ, answered.

A voice whispered.

John staggered.

The voice husked.

John felt weak.

The voice insinuated.

John hung up and slowly, painfully, sat on the first step of the staircase to the second floor where Marsha was standing on the landing, eavesdropping unashamedly on the wall extension in the hall. When he sensed her hovering presence, he looked over his shoulder.

"John."

"Marsha."

"Oh . . . John."

"Oh . . . Marsha."

"John, John."

"Marsha, Marsha."

She swept down the steps and knelt behind him, flung her arms around his neck, and pulled his head back to her bosom. He had forgotten how it felt; he was sorry that he remembered.

"You know," he said dreamily, "when we first met at the Furst family Christmas party in Newport, I thought it would be wonderful that a Furst shall be a Laste. The merging of two great families, the creation of a dynasty, the establishment of a new Establishment." He sighed. "The years passed, we did our conjugal duties, and now all my children are coming home again." He sneered. "The bastards. Well, not technically, but you know what I mean."

Marsha wiped a tear from her cheek on the top of his head, which disgusted him. "I guess we never taught them the right things, John. We certainly never taught them the true meaning of disowned."

Gently he took her wrists and parted her arms from their necklock, stood, turned, took her hands gently and pulled her down the steps to face him. "You realize, of course, what we'll have to do."

Her wrinkled face wrinkled. "Can't we let the Older Deities do it for us? It's so distasteful."

"We have no choice," he answered sternly.

She sighed. "I suppose you're right, as always." A hand plucked at her lace and silk bodice. "You think there's room in here for something from the weapons room?"

Ample, he thought, if you've put your girdle on.

"Well," he said aloud, "we'd better go find out. You wouldn't happen to have something with a bustle on it, would you?"

She giggled as she followed him up to his bedroom. "Oh, John, I got rid of that old thing last year."

Pilandra Eddye was scrubbing and waxing the hall floor, when someone knocked on the door.

She wiped her hands on her apron, wondering who could be calling at this time of night.

She opened the door.

"Oh my god, it's you."

✦3✦

"Be damned and gone to heaven, it really is you," Kent said delightedly, keeping one eye on the winged marble woman, who had fallen over again and was ripping the trunk of a maple tree to shreds as she used it to try to regain her feet.

Chita Juarel, aka housekeeper Hester Kerwin but looking nothing like her in real life, fluffed out her lustrous black hair, ripped off her drab suit skirt to expose the snug jeans she had been wearing underneath all the time, and wiped off her Anglo makeup with her apron to expose the dusky skin beneath the gop. She said nothing.

"I should have known we'd cross paths again."

The marble woman screamed.

Chita grinned.

Quentin and Sheila burst out of the house, hammers and chisels in hand, and collided with each other in amazement when they saw the strange woman no longer dressed in Hester Kerwin's clothes, which hadn't looked half bad on her except they were a little baggy and not her style at all.

Kent, keeping one eye on the marble woman, shrugged. "This is Chita Juarel. An old friend."

Quentin stared.

Sheila poked him for staring.

"We had kind of a war thing a while ago," Chita explained in her faintly Hispanic accent as she hoisted herself agilely onto the railing, straddled it, blinked, then adjusting her ruffles modestly. "Martians and stuff, you know?"

"Martians?" Quentin said.

The marble woman with the wings gave up trying to pull herself up on the tree, which had nearly fallen over anyway, and commenced crawling again. She screamed, too.

"I think," said Kent, "further detailed explanations as to the mysterious reappearance of Miss Juarel into my already hectic life had best be postponed until we've dealt with our stoned friend over there." Thus, he took a hammer from Sheila, who seemed extraordinarily grateful, a chisel from Quentin, who still had one left and so wasn't all that grateful, and moved to the steps.

"Kent," Chita warned. "The inheritance."

"My own film company," he countered.

Chita considered the implications, legally, ethically, and professionally. "I don't see nothing."

Warily, then, and with a certain amount of acute trepidation precipitated by the fact that the marble winged woman had spotted him and was grinning again, with teeth he hadn't noticed before, he took the sagging steps down one at a time, Quentin following cautiously behind. The plan, as he saw it unfold before him, was so simple as to be stupid, which was to chip the creature to death before it crushed them all to unrecognizable pulps which would forever stain the lawn and cause the grass there to turn brown in perpetuity.

It was at that auspicious moment, as he reached the bottom step and the winged marble woman finally reached the lawn, that he truly realized that Maclemmon's evil interstellar plan wasn't a madman's fancy after all. Somehow, either Howie's incantations or the Older Deities' influence over earthly events as they drew ever nearer to their landing zone had wrought unmentionable alterations in the fabric of reality around Hamtucket. He suspected that this creature had been dispatched to soften things up a little.

The notion almost unnerved him, especially when it coupled with the notion that he could actually and with no special effects die here, and produced an offspring of such terror that it made his mother look like a carefree walk in a combat zone.

Perhaps he should reconsider; perhaps he should let Albuquerque have the film company in return for a statue in the park or something. Then he looked at the statue that used to be in the park and was now on his front lawn and decided that a thank-you and God bless you m'lord would do just as well.

"I could play dead," Quentin suggested nervously.

Kent looked at him.

The young man's hands gestured to suit his words. "You know. Play dead. Fall down and let her sniff around me, check me out. Then, while she's distracted, you could sneak up behind her and . . ."

Kent snapped his fingers and brought a brilliant idea to heel. He raced back up the steps, tossed the hammer and chisel aside, ran through the house to the kitchen, ran out the back door, sprinted across the yard to the garage, ran through the door which was luckily open at the time, and ran into the back where, as he suspected, he found a mighty sledgehammer of the type Hamtucketians used to break the ice during the harsh Rhode Island mountain winters. It was damn heavy, and the slightly curved handle bristled with splinters, but he staggered successfully back into the yard, back into the house, back through the house, and back onto the front porch just as Sheila proved her spunky marble mettle by taking a good-size shard out of the creature's left wing as it tried to yank the railing off in order to give it a better way to climb up to the house. The stairs had obviously never occurred to it, since, he reckoned, it had decided that the shortest distance between two points and a baron was a straight lawn.

"Stand back," he ordered.

The creature screamed derisively at the commanding sound of his voice. The porch shook.

Chita stood back. "You think you can lift that thing?"

Grimly Kent gripped the long handle. "Back home we toss telephone poles around for fun."

"Good for you," she said. "You also eat stuff cooked in a sheep stomach."

Quentin, who had remembered in the nick of time that playing dead was supposed to work with bears, not the bizarre minions of Older Deities from beyond the stars, deftly and courageously darted back and forth with his unassuming weapons, keeping the enraged unnatural creature distracted by lopping off more bits while Kent computed trajectory, wind speed, centrifugal force, unless it was the other one, and power of positive thinking, then took a shuddering deep breath and began to spin in a slow but increasingly fast circle.

The huge hammer spun.

Chita cheered him on.

The hammer spun faster.

Quentin chipped.

The winged marble woman screamed her impending triumph hoarsely as she flexed her wings and sent a storm of dusty wind into Kent's eyes.

But Kent persevered, silently apologizing when Chita had to duck, wincing when Sheila dodged out of the way and fell backward into the house, and groaning when the hammerhead slammed mightily into a porch post and nearly brought the roof down.

Even the marble winged woman paused in amazement.

The silence, if it wasn't exactly paradoxically deafening, didn't let anyone hear anything for a while, except for pieces of the porch post pitter-pattering to the ground.

"Well, Bog-Muggoth to hell," Chita swore at the unexpected setback.

Enraged, the winged marble woman screamed at the mention of her interstellar Master and renewed her assault on house and home.

Kent glared his disgust.

Chita shrugged.

Quentin picked Sheila up.

Kent regripped the sledgehammer and tried it again, all the spinning, the turning, the whirling, the whistling of the dented hammerhead whistling through the air, the sighting on the winged marble creature's exposed neck, the inching closer because he had no choice since the pull of the hammer was pulling him closer because of some physical law or other; and finally, with a cry that sent a proud shiver through all sleeping Highlanders everywhere, he stiffened his arms and his resolve and slammed the sledgehammer into the side of the winged marble woman's head.

The handle shattered.

The hammerhead shattered.

The winged marble woman's head didn't shatter, but it fell off.

Silence returned, except for Kent's puffing, Sheila's moaning,

Quentin's swearing, and the winged marble woman's creaking as it staggered headless toward the street, wings fluttering uselessly in a stonelike sort of way.

When at last it collapsed onto the curbing, the neighborhood shook, the curbing shattered, and the maple tree had enough and fell over.

When at last Kent allowed himself to breathe, he noticed that his hands, while stinging like a son of a bitch, were shaking.

When at last Quentin looked fearfully over the railing, he said, "Head's up."

Kent stared in disbelief.

Sheila, however, had had enough of this assault to her senses, her saintliness, and her awareness of life as she used to know it in Rhode Island. She grabbed the hammer and chisel from her boyfriend's fear-numbed hands, vaulted the railing, and disappeared from view.

Kent didn't look.

Chita did, and nodded approvingly before sending Quentin to the garage for a bucket in which to place the newly minted gravel. Then, once they were alone, she turned to Kent and said, "Did you ever think, Lord, you ought to just stick to being a baron or something?"

He grinned.

She grinned.

He blew on his hands and told her that this most likely would only be the first of many instances of unbelievable events prior to the arrival of the Older Deities. He did not want to speculate on what other horrors Howie had had in mind before his mind died with the rest of him.

"You believe me now, don't you?" she said saucily, and with a touch of smug.

"Enough to say that we'd best find that *Bingomomicron* and do whatever it is we're supposed to do to it before it's too late, yes."

"Burn it," she explained.

"Burn it?" Sheila said, climbing the stairs and dusting her hands on her shirt. "Burn it? Do you have any idea what that thing's worth?"

"Do you have any idea what that thing is?" Kent countered.

"No. But if it has anything to do with that thing there, then that thing, the book thing, is worth millions."

He blinked.

Sheila's cheeks flushed with excitement. "Lord, we could sell it to some private collector or consortium of collectors—cash, so we won't have to pay taxes—and we'd each get millions and millions, lots of them. I could—" Her eyes began to fill. "I could afford the best possible care for my slowly dying father, expert rehabilitation for my poor crippled mother, college for my soon-to-be-born niece or nephew, and a lawyer for my addicted and nuts brother." Her tears flowed. "It would be the saving of us all."

"Kent," Chita said, looking at him for guidance and a piece of the action, "what if she's right?"

But Kent had heard that pathos-filled speech too many times before, had seen an innocent young woman just like Sheila corrupted and cast down because greed had fed on her saintly nature in order to allow that saintly nature to care for those she had been a saint to; he also knew the consequences and the prices paid, the souls lost, the heartache engendered; he knew, or would have known if he hadn't been fired right in the middle of the action, how dreams of a better life through the chemistry of avarice too often led to disaster.

Besides, that was then, and this was real life.

"On a cold day in hell," he told her gently.

She screamed.

Chita slugged his arm.

Sheila screamed again.

Chita slapped her.

Sheila slapped her back.

Chita raised a fist, and Sheila grabbed her wrist and raised a fist, and Chita grabbed her wrist, and Kent prudently eased back into the house while the two women struggled for predominance on the porch, one hysterical with saintly grief and exploded expectations, the other trying to slap a little sense into the hysteria that only doubled when Sheila broke away and ran down the steps into the night, ran back up again, and exclaimed, "Jesus, they're coming!"

Kent's heart froze. All that for nothing. His life at an end. No more roles to play, wenches to wench, mothers to avoid, wealth to be modest about. Gone, all gone, because of one madman's insane desire for revenge from beyond the grave.

Damn, he thought.

He hurried back to the porch and looked up at the stars. "Where?" he demanded, as if he had a good idea how to fight them, which he didn't but he wasn't going to let them know because then they'd get even more hysterical than they already were.

"There!" Sheila pointed hysterically.

He looked at a different section of the sky, thought he saw something, realized he wasn't seeing anything, and frowned. "Where?"

Chita tapped his shoulder. "Yo, Lord, lower your sights a little."

He did.

He saw them.

"Shit," Chita muttered. "And I ain't even got them little hot dog things stuck into the roll things yet."

It was then that Kent understood, as he watched the elite of Langford Place step out of their homes and stroll casually toward him, except for one couple who climbed casually into a waiting taxi cab, that the threat of the Older Deities was as nothing compared to the threat of the people who would soon be gathered in his newly inherited house, not only expecting to be fed as decent a meal as one could expect on the last night of the world as they knew it, but also expecting a little entertainment, which would, as he understood it and wished he hadn't, pretty much center around the sacrifice of his baronial body on the altar of their world domination scheme.

Quickly he hustled the women inside and locked the door.

"There. That takes care of that."

Sometimes, he knew, simple is best, what the hell.

"Takes care of what?" Chita asked.

"They don't come in, I don't get sacrificed." He spread his hands.

"They don't come in," Chita said, "they're gonna be pissed."

He shrugged: *So?*

Sheila gasped in understanding. "Then they'll try to break in."

He shrugged: *So?*

There was a knock on the door.

"Don't answer it," Kent ordered.

Chita peered warily through the triangular window, sighed, opened the door to Kent's sudden protests, reached out and dragged Quentin in.

"They're coming," Quentin said as Chita locked the door behind him. He had a bucket in his hand.

Kent, still fuming at Chita's disobedience since it could have been one of *them* in swift and clever disguise and she was damn lucky it wasn't, explained the situation simply and clearly and with a minimum of words and shrugs. Quentin nodded thoughtfully, scowled a little when Sheila explained how they had just lost millions of dollars and probably their only chance for independence from their parents, winced when Chita explained how there wasn't a damn thing to eat in the house, how the hell was she supposed to throw a party, and when it was over, he asked, somewhat timidly on account of his boldness, if perhaps, by burning the dreaded *Bingomomicron* before the guests arrived, they might defuse the situation entirely and go home.

Kent clapped the boy's shoulder. "Excellent, lad, excellent." Eagerly he turned to Chita. "All right, where is it?"

"I don't know."

This, thought Kent, is an expected development.

But it had to be said: "You don't know?"

"What do you think I've been looking for these past two days?" she snapped. "You think I like being a housekeeper in a house that don't have nothing but a mummy case in the attic, no furniture, an old rusted refrigerator in the basement, and a bunch of dust bunnies and cobwebs that don't have no respect for a decent broom? You think I gave up my railroad engineer's job on the Southern Pacific just so—"

Kent grabbed her shoulders.

"Kent," she whispered shyly, "I don't think this is the time, okay?"

"Refrigerator," he said.

"Kitchen," she answered.

"Basement," he said.

"Locked," she answered.

"Basement or refrigerator?" he said.

"Refrigerator," she answered.

"Key?" he said.

"Pocket," she answered.

"Skeleton?" he said.

She nodded.

He nodded.

"Bingo," he said.

"Could be," she answered.

"Door," Quentin said.

"Locked," Kent answered.

"Windows," Sheila gasped.

"Locked," Quentin told her.

"When?" Kent asked.

"Now," Quentin vowed with a triumphant grin, and proceeded to race through all the downstairs rooms, Sheila at his side, locking all the windows and pulling all the shades, while Kent and Chita sprinted into the kitchen, checked to make sure she still had the keys, then opened the door that led to the basement.

At that moment Sheila ran into the kitchen, red-faced and panting. "Do you have any guests?" she asked.

"Not yet," Chita said. Then she pointed to Kent. "Well, him, but he sort of lives here now."

Sheila counted something on her fingers.

Kent watched her, an eyebrow raised, as she counted again on her other hand.

One hand held up four fingers; the other one held up five.

"Oh," she said.

Kent didn't like that. In some instances, "oh" was an expression of surprise, even delight, sometimes even wondrously obscene pleasure; in some instances, "oh" could also be an expression of dismay, or sadness, or disappointment, or resignation, depending upon the circumstance and punctuation; in this instance, however, "oh" sounded more like "uh-oh," which never in his life had ever meant more than one thing.

"Well," he said, "are you going to tell me, or do I have to guess?"

"Don't be snotty," Chita chided.

Sheila looked at the ceiling.

Kent looked at the ceiling even though he didn't want to.

Chita closed the basement door and looked at the ceiling.

"Somebody's up there," Kent said with a sigh that tousled Chita's hair.

Sheila, not at all surprised by his grasp of the situation, nodded fearfully.

"Thumping around, no doubt."

She nodded again.

"It isn't Quentin."

"No," said Quentin from the doorway.

Something rumbled in the basement.

They looked at the floor.

Something thumped upstairs.

They looked at the ceiling.

Kent walked to the counter, opened several drawers and slammed them shut angrily, opened the last one and smiled mirthlessly as he pulled out a cleaver and a butcher knife. "Nobody," he said as he walked to the front hall, the others trailing behind, "had better make one mummy joke, one crack about not opening the mummy case earlier, one comment about how we're all going to die in our beds." He glared over his shoulder. "Not one."

"What beds?" Chita said.

He heard it then—the thumping.

He knew what it was.

He held out the butcher knife for someone to take, without looking to see who would take it.

The sound was the sound of someone, or something, pounding on the inside of the attic door.

No one took the knife.

"We haven't much time," Sheila said, peering through the window beside the door. "Quentin, I'm frightened."

"That's all right, darling," he said, and slipped an arm around her shoulders. "I'll be right here to protect you."

"Oh, Quentin Eddye, my love," she declared lovingly.

He gazed into her eyes. "I love you so."

"Give me the knife," Chita growled.

Kent handed it over and immediately steered her away from the couple and up the stairs.

They didn't have much time.

From the sound of it, the door had begun to splinter.

•4•

The time is near.

All the signs have appeared.

All the pieces are in place.

All that's left now is the celebration.

Wriggling with barely suppressed excitement, the cowled figure slid off the couch onto the floor, scooped up its robe, slipped it on, and scampered trippingly into the kitchen where it expertly prepared a can of tomato soup to break its day-long fast. With milk, not water; water bubbled and steamed, but milk, if handled properly, burned. Though the others would no doubt be feasting lustily in a few minutes, it itself needed no such culinary fortification. Just a light snack, as it were, before the real feast began.

As the soup simmered redly, and perhaps symbolically, on the old-fashioned electric stove, the cowled figure dried off the dangling sleeve that had dragged in the pot, then opened the refrigerator, not without a certain sly sense of irony, and retrieved a bottle of bottled water from the top shelf, poured itself a glass, and sat at the table. It breathed deeply of the tomato and scorch aroma and smiled dreamily; it nearly swooned over the tactile sensations as it crushed duck-shaped soda crackers into its bowl; it chuckled as it anticipated the expressions on the faces of the dedicated faithful when it itself and in person arrived at the height of the sacrifice and showed them what things would really be like when the Older Deities slithered and tentacled and crawled and flew their way into this world.

Then, its bowl filled with crumbs and duck heads, the cowled figure stood, stretched and groaned, stirred the soup, and walked into the front room. Five minutes to dine. Five minutes to kill. Perhaps another quickie prayer session to keep the communication lines open. No. It had learned long ago and the hard way that the Older Deities got really testy when they were bothered too much. Prayers were okay in their place at prayer sessions, but extemporaneous, or even impromptu, supplications were snarled upon.

Perhaps some anonymous calls around the neighborhood, just to see if the dedicated faithful were on their toes. No. A few laughs, maybe, but nothing more, and this was no time for frivolity.

The cowled figure peered around the edge of the black velvet drapery that covered the front window to make sure that the night was still dark and the thick patches of fog were still hanging around.

Perhaps a call to the town to complain about people leaving their statuary strewn all over the street.

Then, with a startled gasp, it tossed back its cowl and widened its eyes.

Its mouth gaped.

Its hand gripped the drapery so tightly, the velvet was crushed.

Was that . . . ?

Could that be . . . ?

Could *he* have actually . . . ?

The cowled figure staggered away from the window, released the drapery just before it tore loose from its rod, tripped over its hem and fell onto the floor, facing in the general direction of the ceiling.

"Bog-Muggoth!" it exclaimed in involuntary interspacial blasphemy. "Ikloxuthi! Omagupchuk!"

Sonofabitch, it thought in more secular terms.

In anger its hand slammed the floor so hard it winced with pain; but it used the pain, and the subsequent fluent interstellar swearing, to clear its mind of needless distractions. To think properly, it had to think; and to think, it had to be unencumbered by the rush of almost orgiastic terror which had sped through its veins when it had seen the Temporary Servant of the Older Deities lying on the lawn, and the curb, and the street.

It had to be able to concentrate.

And as it concentrated, and shook its stinging hand to rid it of the pain which had cleared its mind very nicely, it realized that this was no real setback at all, but a veritable challenge to its skills. For where was the challenge of destroying an enemy, and pretty much the world, if there was no challenge? If that enemy had simply forsaken the inheritance and escaped screaming into the night, it wouldn't have been any fun, much less a challenge.

But Kent Montana had achieved a victory of sorts in the first battle.

It sat up.

It pondered.

Well . . . not really of sorts. The winged marble woman was in actuality dead. That was, to its quick cowled mind, fairly definite. Which made the next round even more delicious in its anticipation. And if, it thought as it hurried to its feet and hurried into the kitchen and hurried to the stove to watch the soup burn, that was the best part about cooking soup . . . and if Montana was killed during those initial skirmishes, it wouldn't hurt things. Not at all. The Older Deities were on their way, nothing short of one simple thing would stop them, and he knew that Montana had neither the brains nor the wit to figure that bit out.

The sacrifice stuff was for the faithful.

The Older Deities already had their sacrifice.

It was called, among other things, Earth.

• • •

The soup burned.

The cowled figure applauded.

It checked its watch and nodded.

Everything was on schedule.

Nothing, but nothing, would stop it now except the unthinkable, which it didn't know about just yet because it was, intrinsically, unthinkable and therefore unknowable and therefore not within its realm of things to think about and remember.

"Bog-Muggoth," it husked affectionately, "I really love this bleedin' shit."

✦5✦

Wasting no time bemoaning and bewailing and trying to figure a last-minute brilliant scheme, Kent and Chita made their way to the second floor, using a swift but unobtrusive stealth honed by experience and enhanced by necessity. Landing by landing. Step by step. Slowly they turned when they reached the top and looked down the rectangular hall toward Kent's room, or the room he would have used if there had been a bed in it and not just his suitcase. To the right of that door was the attic door, and in the dim light of the overhead light Chita turned on with no apologies for not mentioning it earlier, they could see puffs of grey dust billow into the air each time something slammed against it on the other side.

An icy chill raced across the hall and through their bones.

The howling of a wind that wasn't a wind but something else that sounded like the wind howled across the hall and through their bones.

The light dimmed, brightened, dimmed again.

After a hesitation interrupted neither by good sense nor the cavalry, Kent rolled his shoulders vigorously to dispel the tension and loosen the muscles, then sidled along the wall toward the door.

Chita scrambled across the hall and sidled along that wall toward the door.

They stopped when the pounding stopped.

They exchanged glances neither of them really wanted and stared at the door.

It was bulging.

This, thought Kent, is not natural.

As if possessed, or made from some hellishly pliable material most definitely not wood or any of its patented by-products, the center of the attic door began to expand outward, contract inward, and expand outward again. Nothing shattered, nothing splintered, nothing fell off of anything.

The door simply *bulged.*

Kent watched as Chita wiped the blade of the butcher knife against her skirt; he watched as the door continued its bulging as though it were the beat of some horrible heart in the breast of a creature that was the house itself; he watched as his right hand lifted the cleaver in automatic defense, realized what it was doing, and lowered it again.

The wind that wasn't a wind howled.

He inched forward.

The door *bulged.*

He leapt in and out of an empty room with a silent cry, just in case the bulging door was a fiendishly clever diversion and there was instead someone nasty hiding back in the shadows, waiting to pounce upon him and take him prisoner for the coming sacrifice. Once back in the hall, however, he realized how foolish his precipitous action had been. Whatever was behind the door wasn't going to take him prisoner; it was going to skip right to the sacrifice bit without even reading him his rights. He smiled to himself; he smiled over at Chita, who was staring at him as if he'd lost his mind; he smiled when the wind stopped howling and the door stopped bulging.

He stopped smiling when the sound of monstrous footsteps began to echo through the house like the measured beat, beat, beat of a tom-tom, the resonant boom, boom, boom of a drum.

Whatever it was, however, Kent decided it was retreating; the door, for some enigmatic reason, had defeated it.

Given the night, his impending death, the marble stone woman with the wings, and the growing cramp in his left foot, it was a pleasant thought, and he savored it as he groaned and fell against the wall, cursed the cramp and the fact that the stiffness of his western boots would not permit him to massage his instep, his heel, his toes, or anything else that might bring him temporary comfort.

"Point your heel," Chita suggested.

He did, and fell on his ass.

"Not at me," she said. "Baron, sometimes I—"

Suddenly the loud, echoing, menacing footsteps returned, sounding exactly as if the lumbering creature in the attic had merely gone to the farthest wall just to get a running start at the door.

Kent held his breath.

Chita held up the knife and suggested by gestures and incipient hysteria that he get back on his feet in a goddamn hurry, unless his buns were so muscled he could run on them just as fast.

He stood.

The ghostly footsteps came closer.

Louder.

Faster.

Harder.

Until, just as it seemed as if whatever caused those hellish sounds would explode through the door and destroy them all and make his concern over the sacrifice seem awfully trivial . . . they stopped.

He held his breath, pleased that he was getting so good at it.

Silence.

He breathed again, and was doubly pleased he was getting pretty good at that too.

A few seconds later, Chita eased away from her wall, and crouched into an attack position, knife steady in front of her, flashing eyes narrow with suspicion.

Kent watched as she circled the attic door as best she could since she couldn't get behind it, expertly jabbing at the brass knob, the brass keyhole, the brass hinges, the paneled center, the top, the bottom, making small noises in her throat and shifting her weight rapidly and expertly from foot to foot should she need to leap aside and, at the same time, deal a killing blow.

It was fascinating.

But it was also time-consuming, and he of all people understood that time was the one thing he had no time for this night, so he walked over and opened the door.

Chita yelped and slashed at the air.

He peered up into the dark, took the flashlight from his hip pocket and, with a clever signal, told her to follow.

She glared at him in disgust.

He ignored her. She was always glaring at him in disgust. Even in the old days, during the most dangerous hours of the crash-landed Martian's invasion of the world over in New Jersey, when she had stood stalwartly by his side with more weapons hung around her than any one person had a right to carry, much less the strength, she had glared at him in disgust. He reckoned it was her idiosyncratic way of displaying her mild Latin affection for him. At least he hoped it was. He didn't want to think that he actually disgusted her, not after all they'd been through together.

He looked over his shoulder. "Do I disgust you?"

"What?"

"Never mind."

She glared at him in disgust.

He ignored her, and continued up the stairs, one at a time, one foot after the other, until he was able to see over the level of the bare-plank floor.

The attic was empty.

The flashlight's brave but feeble beam proved beyond doubt that the mummy case was still closed.

It also proved that someone, or something, had used the spring-ladder to escape to the roof. He knew this immediately he saw that the spring-ladder was down, and the springs that gave it its name were still vibrating softly. Try as he might, however, he could hear nothing moving on the slates overhead. Was it waiting for him to walk over and look up so it could leap down on his face and flay his flesh to the aristocratic bone? Was it crouching by the chimney, waiting for him to climb the ladder and poke his head out so it could tear his head off and cast it to the wind while nibbling on his baronial brains? Or was it at this very moment already gone, leaping agilely from roof to roof while it plotted sweet revenge for his thwarting its attempt to break down the door, even though he hadn't the faintest idea why the door hadn't broken?

Or had it all been his imagination?

Chita poked him in the small of the back—*git along, little baron, we ain't got all night.*

He moved a few steps more.

Chita came up behind him. "I don't see nothing."

"It's gone."

"What's gone?"

"Whatever tried to get through the door."

"What was it?"

"I don't know. But I do know that I don't want to know. Anyway, it's gone."

"But you don't know what it was."

He shook his head.

"Then how do you know it's gone?"

Valid question, he thought as he swept the room with the beam again, the cleaver back at the ready.

Nothing was there.

"It's gone," he said.

"You sure?"

He nodded.

"Even though you don't know what it looks like, if it's invisible or not, if it's huge or tiny, you're sure it's gone."

He considered the invisible part first, then checked the dusty floor. There were no footprints other than those he had left only a short while ago. Nothing, therefore, had been here since he had been here, and there hadn't been anything there then either.

"Maybe it can fly."

The cleaver quivered.

Chita, however, was emboldened by his declaration of safety and clambered out of the stairwell, looked around in her attack-crouch position and said, "It's gone."

"How do you know?"

"I'm the girl. It don't attack me, it ain't here."

Right, he thought, and followed her to the ladder. They looked at the sky. At the stars. At the glimpse of a vividly green green whirlwind that whirled through the night. A consultation while they looked decided that there was no real need to go up there. If whatever it was was up there, it would kill them trying to climb out; if whatever it was wasn't there, they'd probably fall off the roof without the proper footwear; if whatever it was was still there, waiting, they would fool it by folding the ladder up, scaling the roof, and prevent it from returning. Which, one of them noted, was through the roof via the spring-ladder which, evidently, all it had to do was step on to make it unfold.

They closed it anyway; sometimes physiological reasons that make no sense at all make the best sense of all.

Reluctantly, then, he went next to the Maclemmon mummy case and yanked the lid open without bothering to check for hidden poison needles, attached pinless hand grenades, venomous snakes and/or spiders locked within, powders that produced a lethal gas cloud when dropped into a bowl of water sitting on the bottom, spores that produced lingering diseases often striking only years after the event, or even a spring-and-knife designed to either cut his throat, gouge out his eyes, puncture his liver, or decapitate him.

"Why not?" she asked.

"I didn't feel like it," he told her disdainfully.

"Oh." She nodded. "You forgot."

Before he could muster enough lies to convince her she was wrong, they heard muffled voices and the engine of a taxi cab outside, and Kent realized instantly that this damnable ethereal creature had been only another cunning diversion, one to make them waste precious moments trying to save themselves from an invisible and possibly airborne monster while the dedicated acolytes of the Older Deities gathered for the last ceremony. And if the diversion had killed him, he somehow didn't think the Older Deities would have complained.

"Well," he said, moderately explosively.

Chita looked at the stairwell. "Yes."

"I suppose we'd best get on with it, the burning of the *Bingomomicron* and all."

"Yes," she whispered.

"If we don't succeed, I shall die, you know."

"Yes," she whispered.

Gently, and tenderly, he placed a finger under her chin, turned her face toward his, and smiled ruefully. "Somehow I don't think this will be as easy as the Martian."

Her eyelashes fluttered with melancholy.

His lips grew taut with determination.

Her arms slipped around his neck.

His arms slipped around her waist.

They gazed longingly into each other's eyes.

"Have you noticed," he husked, "how we always manage these priceless moments just before we're going to die in the most horrible manner imaginable?"

"Our nature," she told him, lips moist and quivering. "The tragic Latin and the melancholy Scot. Star-crossed. Ill-fated. Shit like that."

He sniffed. "Well, I wouldn't say ill-fated exactly." He managed a brave smile. "There was the Martian egg nest, remember."

She frowned.

He was aghast. "You . . . forgot?"

She grinned.

He smiled.

She said, "You remember the first time you really saw me? just before the building blew up?"

He did. She had been naked.

"So, you wanna fool around now or later?"

He sighed. "Now. But it'll have to be later, I'm afraid."

"I know." She pouted pleasantly. Kissed him quickly. "Your loss, gringo."

Of course, he thought as she bounded down the stairs; there's always a goddamn catch.

He was checking his hair again when, without warning, she bounded back up the steps.

"You wanna die up here where it's all dirty?"

"I don't want to die anywhere," he said stiffly, and followed her back to the second floor. "In fact, I don't plan to die for quite some time, thank you very much."

"Not your plan," she reminded him ungraciously. "It's Howie's."

Then someone knocked on the door.

The downstairs door, Kent told her scornfully when she crept back out of the room that would have been his bedroom had there been a bed in it and not just his suitcase. And then, right then, there was no longer time to stall, no longer time for regrets, no longer time to stall, no longer time to formulate contingencies and back-ups and fall-backs and escape hatches and stalling techniques.

No time for anything, not even stalling.

He just hoped there was time to burn the damn book.

"What happened?" Quentin asked as they hurried to the first floor and back toward the kitchen.

"Don't ask," Kent called over his shoulder. "Just stay here and keep watch."

"For what?"

"We don't know, it's invisible," Chita said.

"It's what?"

"Invisible."

"Oh Jesus," Quentin moaned, "I'm dead."

"Again?"

"What?"

Kent, determined to keep the rest of his dwindling sanity intact, refused to listen to the rest. Instead, he hefted the cleaver and wondered if he ought to bring it with him wherever he was going. He already had a gun. The cleaver might be overdoing it. Unless wherever he was going had something bullets couldn't stop but a blade could. On the other hand, if bullets couldn't stop it, he'd have to get close enough to use the blade, and he wasn't at all sure he wanted to get close enough to something that only a blade could kill.

If the blade could kill it.

If it couldn't, maybe he could deafen it with screams.

Chita, meanwhile, boldly, and without asking permission, pushed past him and opened the basement door, flicked on the light—a single pastel bulb flickering weakly in a pear-shaped chandelier—and started down the rickety wooden steps. Kent followed, but not as eagerly because, no matter how hard he tried, he knew that this whole thing was too easy. Just going down into a dusty, dirty, low-ceiling, exposed-beam, hard-dirt-floor basement and burning a book was too damn easy.

He didn't want to think it.

He thought it anyway: there's a catch.

God, he hated that.

On the other hand again, maybe it was about bloody time he had it easy when it came to saving his life and the lives of those around him, and the world too, in the bargain, which wasn't much of one when one thought about it; maybe, just maybe, complications like a well-dressed mob out to sacrifice him weren't going to matter anymore; it was entirely possible that a simple burning match to a not so simple Mystical Book of Evil would take care of everything and let him inherit the inheritance without a lot of fuss and bother and hospital costs. Of course, the marble woman with the wings had been a bother, no question about it, and the thing that had maybe been in the supposedly empty attic too, but nothing was *that* simple, let's be realistic here.

Yes, it was time.

High time.

"Shit," said Chita Juarel.

And Kent dragged himself kicking and screaming back to the real world, where the basement had a hard-packed dirt floor, the walls were concrete and darkly stained from leaking, the beams were exposed and rotting before his very eyes, and there were benches and tables along the back wall, littered with rusting, rusted, and about to disintegrate tools and other things which he hadn't the stomach to check out.

The real world.

Where the thirty-year-old, once-white refrigerator door with the rounded corners was open, and from deep within came a pulsing, throbbing, vibrating, winking, blinking, fluid, beating, palpitating green light.

Also, a lot of muffled growling, echoing as if from the bottom of a well.

"Hey, Lord," Chita said, shading her eyes with one hand, her voice soft in awe and terror, "you want to know what's in here?"

"No," he begged. "Please."

"A tunnel."

"Jesus Christ." He shook his head, scratched his brow, rolled his eyes. "A tunnel to another world, I've no doubt. The very tunnel the Older Deities are going to use to enter this world."

"Nope," she contradicted. "Looks like it goes next door."

He frowned, then tried to orient himself vis-a-vis the numerals he had seen on the houses he had seen on the block he was on. "You mean . . . to Number 670?"

She turned away from the pulsing and throbbing and vibrating and beating green light. "I don't think so."

Of course not.

A threatening shadow appeared at the top of the basement stairs, blocking the light from above.

Kent whirled, the cleaver ready to throw.

The shadow leaned down. "Mr. Montana?"

He relaxed. "Yes, Sheila?"

"Someone's knocking at the door."

Naturally.

"Well, don't answer it."

"But they're knocking."

"Sheila," he said, summoning patience as if it were a demon. He stopped. He rubbed his nose. He moved to the foot of the stairs and looked up. "Sheila, have you been paying attention to what's going on here tonight?"

She held up a hand. "Please. I'm not stupid."

"I didn't say you were."

"But someone's knocking."

"You're an idiot."

"Kent," Chita chided.

Sheila wept loudly, maintaining that her innate goodness and strict upbringing had always taught her to answer the door, answer the telephone, and change her poor struggling father's oxygen tanks once every three hours. What the hell was she supposed to do, change her whole life overnight?

The green light pulsed more strongly.

"Kent," Chita warned.

"Do not answer the door," he told the girl kindly. "Be strong. Lean on Quentin. He knows what's best."

"He wants to answer the door."

And Chita said, "Kent, bring that cleaver over here. I think there's something moving in there."

•6•

Wally Putney, his loving slut of a wife clinging elegantly, and somewhat chastely, to his left arm, strolled up Langford Place in the brisk night air. It was a lovely evening, as an inarguable matter of fact. Those fog patches over there added just the right touch of October mystery, the breeze brought just the right hint of harvest and Halloween, the trees were rustling, the leaves were rustling, the neighborhood dogs and cats except for Puffball were on their nocturnal prowls.

It was wonderful.

"Wally," Caroline agreed with a sigh and contented squeeze of his arm.

The sight of old, kindly, monumentally ugly Dr. Smith hobbling down his steps, and the sparkling vision of John and Marsha Furst-Laste slipping richly out of their taxi, nearly made him forget, though he could never really forget, the telephone call that threatened to ruin it all.

He shook himself.

That particular bridge would be surveyed, constructed, and

crossed when he came to it. For now, there were far more important matters to deal with.

"Did you bring the cards?" he asked.

Caroline patted her spangled purse lovingly.

Good.

Dr. Smith spotted him and waved.

The Putneys returned the wave gaily and moved quickly up the street toward him, noting that for some reason he had decided to bring along his hand-sewn black medical bag. Wally figured it was a sensible precaution against peripheral injuries during the sacrifice and landing; Caroline hoped it wasn't because Wally's former spouse formerly thought charred to cinders at the bottom of a ravine had somehow let her intentions be known to more than just Wally.

"Nice night," Smith said, breathing deeply.

"Beautiful," Wally agreed, breathing deeply.

Caroline breathed deeply.

"Hello there," Marsha Furst-Laste called from across the street after the taxi had driven away.

"Hello," Wally called. "You certainly look lovely tonight."

Dr. Smith chuckled. "A face like that needs a good ironing."

Caroline tsked with a giggle.

John Laste, who had never been hyphenated in his life, including Harvard English, waited patiently on the sidewalk, hands clasped before him, hair stirring gently in the breeze without getting mussed. Marsha stood beside him and beckoned the others over.

"Ah well," sighed Dr. Smith. "Time to get moving, I suppose."

"Absolutely," Wally answered with proper solemnity. And as he crossed the street he looked at the shade-darkened windows of Number 668. "It would seem that Mr. Montana has other ideas." He smiled.

"Let him," Smith grumbled. "He's a foreigner. He doesn't know how things work over here."

"Well, so was Maclemmon," Wally pointed out.

"But he's dead."

Wally paused with raised eyebrow: "Is he?"

Before Smith could question that enigmatic verbalization, Wally held out his hand and strode to John, who shook the offered hand solemnly.

"Wally."

"John."

"Wally, dear."

"Marsha."

"Marsha!"

"Caroline."

"Caroline!"

"John."

"Evening."

"Dr. Smith."

"Kenilworth!"

"Caroline."

A wolf howled in the distance.

Wally stepped out of the welcoming pack and glanced around the deserted street. The houses were dark, the shadows clumped around the feeble streetlamps and gathered on empty porches. He shivered a little, but steeled himself against the coming ordeal. This was no time to display weakness.

No time at all.

Dr. Kenilworth Smith glared at the way the others greeted each other so familiarly, so correctly, so damn smugly. As if they were absolutely convinced that nothing would dare disturb the celestial forces gathering here this momentous night. As if Montana's inept and futile closing of the house were nothing more than a moth to be crisped in the flame of their greedy passions. As if he, the only practicing physician within blocks, were nothing but a peripheral character who carried a black bag instead of a spear. As if they would not, at the last, be on their knees and begging for his help.

It was enough to make him laugh; so he did, and did not apologize when they all looked at him for an explanation of his apparent levity on such a solemn occasion, which was getting too damn solemn for his taste. But they never asked his opinion about anything, did they? Never. They just assumed he would be there when they needed him. Good old ugly kindly Dr. Smith. The patient's best friend. The trusted confidant of the halt and lame. The procurer of legal drugs. The man who was older than he looked who lived smack in the middle of the block and was always on call when they, the scum, suddenly required the services of a healer.

It was enough to make him puke.

He didn't; he had his limits.

Instead, he suggested tartly that they stop their mutual admiration society group grope and get on with it because, unless he was badly mistaken, and he'd never been sued in his life, there was a faint green glow swirling now and again in the autumn sky, and they all knew what that meant.

A prolonged silence was their response, which, of course, was meant to tell him that they already knew that, and that civilized people simply were not rushed into such earth-shattering, as it were, matters.

It was then that Dr. Smith, keen on observation and pretty good at it too, noticed that the Lastes were doing their best to conceal a certain apprehension which, he divined, had nothing to do with tonight's events.

He also noted how Caroline Putney clung so possessively to Wally's flabby arm, as if they were attempting to camouflage beneath a show of spousal affection an anxiety that pertained not at all to the evening's schedule.

Curious.

There was more here than meets the eye.

Suddenly Marsha gasped, clasped one hand to her bosom, pointed with the other one, and said, "Who is that?"

"Why . . . I don't know," her husband answered stiffly.

"Why," Wally said, "it's—"

"Pilandra!"

Well, thought Pilandra Eddye nervously, here we come; walking down the street. Bold as brass and twice as stupid. She saw the others staring and looked up at her companion.

"We get the funniest looks from everyone we meet, have you noticed that?"

"Hey," her companion said softly. "Hey, we're the monkeys in this little zoo, Pilandra. Free entertainment for the carnivorous snobs who think themselves lions and tigers and panthers and such."

She did her best not to giggle.

It was true.

The Putneys and the Furst-Lastes and Dr. Kenilworth Smith couldn't have looked more disapproving if she had danced naked in broad daylight in the middle of the street. Not that they hadn't seen her naked before, some of them, but that was another story. That had nothing to do with tonight's ceremonies which they thought she had nothing to do with but had more to do with than they thought.

Her companion touched his eye patch absently, then pushed a strong hand through his flowing blond hair.

How wonderful, how frightening, how coincidental, how cosmic, she thought with wonder and delight, that he of all people should return to her dreary life after being absent for so long without explanation or postcard. For indeed it was he, Rex Regal presently in disguise, who had previously stepped into her drab and uneventful mundane existence after her foreman husband had tragically drowned in the ice cream factory refrigerator meltdown, saving all the other workers before thinking of his own life and leaving her damn near destitute, the thoughtless, potbellied little bastard; yes, Rex Regal, who had shown her the sweet mysteries of life and how at last she found them; Rex Regal, who was in truth—

"Pilandra," John said unctuously and politely. "How . . . kind of you to join us."

But she saw them all staring at Rex, wondering who he was, admiring his muscles, measuring his tuxedo, coveting his hair. It made her grin.

"It was Howmaster's wish," she said humbly.

"I'm quite sure it was," Wally said, jumping into the awkward pause and nearly breaking his ankle. He limped a little as he turned his wife toward the house. "And I'm sure Howmaster wouldn't want us to spend the rest of our ordinary lives hanging around street corners and gossiping."

They laughed appreciatively.

And sobered instantly when, in the autumn sky above them, they saw a brief whirlwind of intensely green green soar between the stars.

In the sky above Hamtucket, astronomers, who weren't actually in the sky but taking a good look at it from places more grounded, photographed and witnessed and otherwise scientifically recorded the curious sight of an intensely green green whirlwind whirling between the stars.

It made them nervous.

Some of that green seemed to have claws.

• • •

Caroline snuggled closer to her husband as they approached the front walk of the house that was to change their lives forever if they didn't screw things up, as the children might say. Yet she wasn't as nervous about the upcoming rites and bloodletting as she was about the handsome stranger who had magically appeared in Pilandra Eddye's life. There was something about him so familiar, so close to the tip of her tongue, so near and yet so far, that she couldn't control a chilled fluttering in her stomach. Why, it almost made her feel as if she had committed adultery in her heart, and she didn't even know the man.

If it hadn't been for Wally's former wife previously thought long dead lurking somewhere back there in the shadows, or over there under that tree, or down there in the street—no, that was Ivan—or up there on that widow's walk, she might even be tempted to explore these feelings further. As it was, she was forced to play the dutiful wife and sacrificer as if nothing was wrong. It would be difficult. She would do it.

She was, after all, a Putney.

A trio of elegantly attired somewhat elderly gentlemen looked up at the sky with some apprehension.

"Well," said the tallest one, "I think it's time we headed back, don't you?"

"Oh yes, yes," agreed the shortest one, rubbing his hands together.

The middle-size one shrugged his supreme disinterest and popped a jelly bean into his mouth.

"Then," said the tallest one, "shall we?"

They turned.

And he only hoped and prayed that they hadn't walked so far away from where they were destined to be that they wouldn't be able to walk back in time. As it was, he was already puffing a little, a sure sign that he was getting tired. And if he got tired, if he was forced to stop for a rest however brief, Kent Montana was, in an ominous word, doomed.

John hung back unnoticed as the others climbed the stairs in grim but companionable silence.

Although, at first glance, it seemed impossible, it appeared from the lack of reaction on the part of his compatriots that he was the only one who had noticed that the drunken headless woman with the chipped wings lying in the street, and on the lawn, was actually the awful marble statue from Langford Park. He understood immediately the significance of the distressing debris, and for the first time since this whole affair—the Howmaster Maclemmon one—began, he felt a brush of doubt sweep across his heart.

If a mere actor, albeit a Scots baron, had been able to dispatch one of the Older Deities' Unnatural Servants on Earth with such evident dispatch, it seemed to John that the mere mortals now clumped like well-appointed cattle at the front door weren't going to be any problem at all, dispatch-wise. And that was an unexpected problem, because there weren't supposed to be any problems, unexpected or otherwise, or at least none they wouldn't be able to handle without any problem.

Bog-Muggoth, he prayed with head momentarily bowed and even though he knew the Older Deities hated casual contact, if You know what's going on here, I wish You'd tell me so Marsha doesn't get her girdle all in a bunch, You know how she is about things not going as planned.

He waited.

There was no answer.

Kthulkucuth, are you listening? Sazrihanaz? Azmedium? Ghiumoshikh?

Nothing.

He sighed and straightened his cuffs.

As always, the Older Deities were leaving such trivial matters to him to take care of. As always. Even when Howmaster had been alive and foaming, it had been none other than John who had to make sure the street didn't know what was happening under its very collective nose; it had been none other than John who had used his masculine wiles to see to it that the women didn't fuss about womanly things instead of things that really mattered; and it had been good old reliable John who had clubbed his former wife over her head and released the hand brake that sent that little sports coupe plummeting into the ravine to explode in a ball of flame that—

Stop! he ordered; stop!

"John, dear?"

He smiled at his wife, touched his jacket to be sure the perfect weapon was still there, noticed that the others were touching themselves in curious places too, and took a deep breath to gather his resources.

"My friends," he said with a satiric smile, "I do believe I'm hungry."

"Damn right," Dr. Smith growled.

"Perhaps Mr. Montana . . ." His smile became a feral grin. "Perhaps Mr. Montana is ready now to receive us." He climbed the steps and looked at Wally. "Mr. Putney, if you would be so kind as to open the door?"

Wally nodded at the honor, took the knob in hand, braced himself, and turned it.

"It's locked," he said.

"I see," said John. Lord, he was so weary of all these puny obstacles. "Then perhaps you would be so kind as to break one of the windows there, climb in, come around, and unlock the door so that we might enter in the proper manner?"

Wally tenderly disengaged his wife's clinging hand from his arm, walked over to one of the high windows, and said, "The shade's down."

"Yes," John said, "it is."

"There might be a trap on the other side."

"It's entirely possible, Wallace, entirely possible. Mr. Montana, for all that he is an actor, albeit a Scots baron, is clearly not a stupid man."

"I mean, John, that since he is, we've all agreed, a clever man, there could be a guillotine blade in there, or broken glass all over the floor, or a shotgun tied to the back of a chair or something like that."

Dr. Smith hugged his black bag to his chest. "Jesus, just break the glass, Wally. Go for it."

"Easy for you to say. You've got the bandages."

John fluttered his eyes shut and prayed for strength as only the rich can when faced with people who were also rich, but stupid too.

Then, from out of nowhere:

"Be . . . ware."

They turned as one, the women gasping as usual, the men scowling.

Ivan Vlaskovich, ironing board at the ready, pointed a quivering, half-gloved finger at them. "Be . . . ware the door locked from the inside, for that door is locked and shall not be opened."

"We know that," said John coldly.

"Ah."

"And it's locked."

Ivan shrugged expressively. "Told you that already. You wouldn't listen. Not my problem." He wandered away, into the night, into the patchy fog.

There was a silence again.

"Well," said the familiar stranger with Pilandra Eddye, "I hope you won't mind if I break it in then?"

John shook his head.

The familiar stranger moved away from the door, braced his arm against his side, aimed his shoulder, and fairly vibrated with the energy he sent thrumming into his powerful legs as he prepared to launch himself at the door's center.

"Someone's coming," Marsha said, her ear to the door, her eye on the familiar stranger so she could duck away in time not to get smashed.

The familiar stranger launched.

The door opened.

Ivan walked by in the other direction and called out to John: "I could have told you that, too. You don't listen, that's not my problem."

And Chita Juarel, looking down the hall toward the blond blur now approaching the kitchen, said, "Hey, who was that patched man?"

- VII -

The Guiding Light

✦1✦

There were any number of repugnant and repulsive aspects to basements throughout the civilized world; so many, in fact, that Kent was at least as unenchanted by them as he was by attics; perhaps more so. Basements brought to mind dungeons. Dungeons brought to mind the cold and rainy winter afternoon he had explored the one he'd discovered below the basement of his family manse. He had been quite young then, and unaware that getting into the dungeon from the basement had been altogether far too easy for one of such tender years.

He almost didn't get out.

And when he did get out, his astonished nanny punished him for soiling his clothes by crawling around the basement without permission. What she did was lock him in the dungeon. Harsh, perhaps, but the stay stood him in good stead in future since it enabled him to practice his escaping skills to such an extent that, by the time he was nine, his mother had given up all hope and had the dungeon walled up except for the secret door beneath the roses in the greenhouse.

Thus, although no one noticed, it was a far, far better thing that Kent did, standing in the basement by himself and not screaming, than he had ever done before, which was scream.

He stood now in front of the ominously innocuous refrigerator and stared at the door stained with stains that defied identification, although he had a pretty good idea what some of them were. Chita had closed it before she'd gone upstairs; he didn't want to reopen it. Nothing good ever happened when you opened a refrigerator when you weren't supposed to. Even when you're a kid, you open a refrigerator door to see what's inside that you might want to snack on and all the cold gets out, your mother wants to know if you're trying to air-condition the kitchen, and before you can think of a decent excuse it's a weekend back in the dungeon with milk, stale biscuits, and Nanny to show you how the Iron Maiden works; not that she was all that pliable herself.

But if he didn't go in there, and without further delay, uncover the source of the pulsing green light, then find the dreaded, legendary *Bingomomicron* and burn it, he would have to return upstairs and meet the new neighbors gathering on the porch. From the sounds of it, they weren't in a terribly good mood. Even if they had been in a rousing good mood, he reminded himself as he reached for the handle, he probably wouldn't want to meet them anyway because they wanted to kill him.

It was so difficult sometimes to understand Americans.

Nevertheless, it was one of those times for a major decision which, with any luck, he wouldn't have to make.

Quentin hovered uncertainly at the foot of the staircase. "Are you sure you want to go?"

"Bloody hell, of course I don't want to go," Kent snapped irritably.

The young man shrugged as if he didn't see any problem, moral or otherwise. "Then don't go."

"Oh, yes," Sheila agreed. "Don't."

They make a lot of sense, he thought.

An abrupt burst of thundering footsteps above made him glance in alarm toward the rough-hewn, rotting beams; a sudden crash and tinkling of shattered glass made him stare at the basement door; a subsequent stream of freshwater curses that made Sheila blush, clear as they were through the floor and the door, made him decide that he did not want to meet the man who had done whatever had been done up there. Oddly enough, his state of mind—extreme emotional turmoil and immoderate unease—made the ruckus sound as if some drunken fool had run at top speed through the length of the building and smashed through the back door, but something like that only happened in the movies. Chita, he reckoned, had probably beat the shit out of someone who had tried to play house with its keeper.

More footsteps.

Chita's muffled voice in a query, and someone responding rather formally.

The ghost of the unearthly chilled wind he had felt so clearly in the upstairs hall just before he discovered that there wasn't anything in the attic making all that noise drifted through the basement, swaying cobwebs and emotions, and raising gooseflesh on his arms.

A glistening fat spider paused on a narrow splintered beam overhead and checked him out for possible suburban renewal. Without any entomological training at all, he noticed that the plump-bodied, long-limbed arachnid was green. Neon green. Like the one he had spotted in the back parlor earlier that evening. This one, however, had a much more aggressive stance, a red stripe across its bulbous head, and protruding black eyeballs that seemed to watch him with such intensity that he was instantly reminded of one of his babysitters, the fat hairy one with the cape and tight pants who had been imported from the north of Spain, and who wanted to play bullfight with him and kept trying to get him to say "Moo." Kent, already wise to the ways of his imported babysitters, fashioned a pair of horns from Cook's carving set. The fat hairy Spaniard lasted less than a week, and the stains were out of the carpet by Thursday.

Seconds passed.

The spider waved a hairy leg and scrambled away.

Kent experienced no relief; he knew this was only another harbinger, one of those damn portent things that portended bigger, uglier, deadlier spiders to come.

All right, all right, make up your mind, man, he ordered himself sternly; dithering is one of your strong points, but it won't save your life this time.

And having finally made up his mind, he wished he hadn't but there was no turning back now. The Thespian had given way; the Baron was now in charge. The idiot.

He waited for the organ.

It played not a single note.

Nuts; it would have been a nice touch. Fanfare in B-flat for Titled Moron and Funeral.

"Quentin," he said, using all the bravado and bluster he could muster under the about to be dire circumstances, "stay down here, if you would, please. Make sure no one follows me into the refrigerator. Bash them if they try."

Quentin was clearly awed. "But sir, surely you're being needlessly brave."

Tell me about it, he thought grumpily; but I don't see you volunteering to be the Hamtucket idiot.

"But I'll do my best."

"All I can ask," Kent told him.

Quentin barely managed a smile.

Kent adjusted his cardigan, hitched up his belt, polished his boots on the back of his jeans.

"It's been an honor to meet you, sir."

Kent glanced at him and nodded. "I'm not dead yet, you know."

Quentin blinked in confusion. "Oh, I didn't mean that. Really. I was just saying that it's been an honor to meet you, that's all."

"Okay."

Kent pulled out the gun, and checked to be sure it was loaded.

"Just in case . . . you know."

"Cork it," Kent said quietly as he hefted the cleaver several times to be sure it hadn't suddenly turned into rubber.

"Can I have your suitcase?"

Kent glared.

Quentin backed away hastily, mimed zipping his lips shut, and bowed his head.

Praising himself for great strength of character that left the boy still breathing without artificial means, Kent turned away, puffed his cheeks, blew a breath, whispered an ancient Gaelic prayer for strength and a clearly marked exit, and slowly, gingerly, opened the refrigerator door, bracing himself for a lordlike leap into the middle of Connecticut in case some awful, indescribable monster charged him from the uncharted depths of the freezer compartment.

There was nothing in there, however, but the omnipresent green light, pulsing preternaturally into the room, turning everything within its reach an ominous shade of red.

He noted instantly that the light wasn't nearly as strong as it had been when Chita had first discovered it, nor did there seem to be anything shifting and sneaking around in there, setting up a monstrous ambush. In fact, when he leaned closer and examined the way more carefully, all he could see was a crude, plank-and-beam supported, hand-excavated tunnel beginning where the back of the refrigerator ought to be. It appeared to be fairly straight, if a bit rugged, and because the light emanated from the as yet invisible far end, he could see just about everything in between, including the bleached bones of small animals scattered on the dirt floor, and the horned skull of a charging rhino loosely nailed to one wall. At that point he regretted not bringing the family claymore as well, but it was difficult enough getting it into the suitcase's secret compartment, much less hauling it through airport security. They tended to question things like that these days, more's the pity.

I do not want to go in there, he told anyone who may have been psychically eavesdropping; I have seen places like this before, and they fall down on people just when they least expect it, burying them forever in an unmarked tomb of dust and rock. They even write songs about them.

A muffled thumping and scraping from above distracted him, and he glanced over his shoulder. "Sheila, go up and help Chita deal with those people."

"Who?"

"Chita."

"Chita who?"

"Chita Juarel," he answered patiently. "The one who used to have brown hair and now has black hair? Kind of curly?" He waited. "She has an accent?" He waited. "The housekeeper?"

The young woman wrinkled her brow in puzzlement, looked at Quentin, and nodded. "Oh. Miss Kerwin."

"Her name isn't Kerwin. It's Juarel. Remember?"

"Okay, whatever," she said brightly, kissed Quentin's cheek cheerily, and skipped up the steps. Paused at the door and said, "What am I supposed to do to help her?"

He looked at his gun, at the edge of the cleaver's blade, and reminded himself that what he was thinking about doing just wasn't done. Well, it was done, but it wasn't legal. "Serve the food, make them laugh, how the bloody hell should I know? just don't let them down here, do you understand? No matter what, keep them upstairs."

"Then what am *I* doing here?" Quentin wanted to know, hefting a dull hatchet he'd discovered rusting on a bench at the back of the room.

"Protecting my back," Kent said, "in case someone comes down."

"What?" Sheila pouted and stamped her foot in a fit of pique she scraped off daintily on the step. "You just told me not to let anyone down here, didn't you? What's the matter, don't you trust me to follow a simple instruction like don't let anybody down here?" She shook her head wearily. "He doesn't trust me, Quentin, I can tell. I don't know why I bother. All the work and no thanks, that's what I always get. Sheila do this, Sheila do that. Like the time Father tried to ignite—"

"Darling, he trusts you, honestly," Quentin assured her quickly. "Don't you trust her, Kent? Of course he does. I can see that. Really."

"Then," she said, brightening, while someone else shattered something else up there in the kitchen, "why don't you come with me?"

"Because I have to stay here."

Immediately, Kent bent over and stepped hastily into the potentially treacherous, unused refrigeration unit, less because he wanted to and more because if he didn't, he'd probably do something drastic enough to put him behind bars for an unnaturally long time. As it was, he could still hear them debating their positions relative to the possible end of the universe and the basement staircase as he moved warily out of the refrigerator's porcelain bowels and into the tunnel, his eyes protesting the waning strength of the green glow, his gun hand twitching every time he thought he heard a noise.

Then, less than ten feet away from the entrance at Number 668, he was abruptly enveloped in silence. No voices, no breaking of whatever had been broken, and nothing even slightly hinting at unnamable horrors from ahead.

He supposed it was a good sign; he supposed he ought to have his head examined.

He moved on.

Moisture dripped in cold droplets from the ceiling. Puddles formed darkly on the uneven floor. Scurrying dark things scurried in and out of shadows formed by the bulks of great jagged boulders protruding at odd angles from the walls. He imagined there were rats in the walls as well, and couldn't help a violent shudder. He didn't like rats. They revolted him. It stemmed from the time some years ago when his mother had imported a herd of them from Norway and tried to train them to bring grenades into his bedroom during the night. Luckily, the little buggers kept playing with the pins she'd smeared with fresh cheese, thus saving his life on more than one occasion, but wreaking havoc and holes on the family manse foundation.

He moved on.

A faint rumbling rumbled trainlike through the tunnel, and he froze as bits and clots of moist dirt pattered softly from the ceiling. The green light flickered. He prayed that whatever caused it wouldn't lose power. If it did, he'd be in the dark; not that he fully understood everything anyway, but dark is dark when there is no light, and he'd just as soon forgo the experience.

The rumbling stopped; he moved on.

And when he finally saw the outline of the end of the tunnel, he began to wish he had more than one life to live, just in case; and, simultaneously, another way to put it. One life had a decidedly macabre and permanent ring to it. For some reason it made him think of a fragile soap bubble, bouncing briefly in the breeze before bursting and vanishing.

Charming, he thought; keep it up, then cut your throat, why not.

He moved on.

Sheila marveled at the way Chita, or Hester, adroitly assembled the guests in the back parlor without bruising their egos or thighs. Though they stared a little disconcertedly at the little folding chairs with the stenciled robins and chickadees, and silently questioned Chita's snug jeans and ruffled shirt, they said nothing as they took their assigned places; why, it's almost as if it had all been rehearsed.

My heavens, she thought; could it really be? Have I really been that blind to everything that's been going on around here right under my nose?

It was a sobering thought.

The organ thought so too.

The elegant and a little scary Mr. Laste sat with his back to the fireplace, clearly the leader and clearly a man who got what he wanted when he wanted it. That impressed her. She wondered if she could convince him to want her father. Or her mother. Her brother, she figured, was a lost cause, and somebody had already wanted her sister, and got her.

She herself had been tapped by the housekeeper who wasn't really a housekeeper to find enough glasses so that the guests would be able to have their choice of drinks, as long as it came from the tap in the kitchen sink.

They didn't complain, however, not even when she returned a second later, did her best to curtsy the way she had seen the Danish maids do on *Passions and Power,* and told them there weren't any glasses.

"It is of no consequence," Mr. Laste said understandingly, smiling at the others. "I think we'll survive."

The others murmured their agreement.

Except, Sheila noted, for Quentin's mother. She sat near the windows, next to a man with a towel wrapped around one shoulder and a patch on one eye. He was undoubtedly one of the handsomest men she'd ever seen in her short, cloistered life; yet there was something familiar about him, so teasingly so that she couldn't stop staring.

"You got a problem?" Chita whispered harshly as she rushed out of the room.

Sheila followed her into the kitchen. "That man."

"Which one?"

"With the patch."

"What about him?"

"He's familiar."

"Sure he is," Chita said matter-of-factly as she reached into a brown paper bag and pulled out a box of crackers, a tin of sardines, and a red-rimmed paper platter. "He looks just like your boyfriend."

Sheila gasped.

The organ recovered its voice.

Chita turned to her slowly. "Say. You're not thinking . . . ?"

But Sheila yanked open the basement door, looked down at Quentin looking back up at her with an expression of *now what?,* slammed the door with a muttered apology, ran into the dining room and stared into the back parlor. All heads turned toward her. She stepped timidly into the room. All eyes watched her. Her lips tried a smile as she crossed the bare floor and stood in front of the man wearing the patch. She looked from him to Mrs. Eddye. To him again. To Mrs. Eddye.

"Oh my heavens," she whispered, and ran out of the room, into the kitchen, yanked open the basement door and stared down at Quentin, who looked up frowning until she slammed the door again and fell against it, panting.

"So what do you think?" Chita asked.

"I think," said Sheila Verlin in a voice much older than her two-score years, "things are going on on this block that I don't know what's going on."

"You just figured that out?"

"Well, I had a thought a couple of minutes ago, but in general . . ." She nodded.

"You been sniffing your old man's oxygen too much, that's what."

Sheila gasped hoarsely. "How did you know?"

Chita gaped. "What?"

"Please," Sheila begged, "don't tell Quentin. He thinks I'm a saint. He doesn't know about . . . my addiction."

"No problem. I do too."

Sheila gasped. "You do? I mean, you are? Addicted to oxygen, I mean?"

Chita stared at her for a very long time. "Tell me," she said at last. "How long has Quentin been dead?"

My god, thought Pilandra Eddye in barely controlled consternation; oh my god, she *knows*!

Wally Putney said nothing when the strange girl ran out of the room in an equally strange panic, but he couldn't help but notice when Pilandra clapped a hand to her cheek in horror. Then he realized how clever that Sheila person had been. All the time she had been staring at the familiar stranger, she'd actually been staring at *him*.

My god, he thought as Pilandra struggled for a breath; oh my god, she *knows*!

Dr. Kenilworth Smith wondered if the girl really *knew* all she seemed to know. If she did, really, all hell would break loose; if she didn't, all hell would break loose anyway, considering the arrival of the Older Deities and all. Nevertheless, he had to be sure.

"My dear," he said to Pilandra, "you look as if you've seen a ghost."

A ghost? thought Caroline Putney in utter horror and anticipation of humiliation. Oh my god, he *knows*!

John Laste sensed that this most momentous of meetings was rapidly slipping away from his control. Everybody was staring at everybody else, slapping themselves on the cheek, and gaping with horror. It might have been amusing if the timing had been better; as it was, he nearly jumped from his ridiculous little chair with the robins and chickadees every time he heard a car drive by the house, thinking it might be *them,* returning to claim their rightful place in the family archives.

"Excuse me," he said loudly, and had to say it several times before he could regain their attention. "Don't you think we'd better get on with the ceremony?"

"But what about Kent Montana?" Marsha asked in that maddeningly pragmatic way she had when she was being utterly practical.

"What about him?"

"He's not here."

"I can see that, my dear. He's in the basement, if you remember. We can fetch him when it's time."

She sat back, not entirely convinced.

He stared at her staring at Caroline with a look that made Caroline stare back at her, then at him, then at her husband, then at the floor where a neon green spider vanished between the planks.

Control, he thought; I must maintain control.

"Kthulkucuth," he intoned.

"Bog-Muggoth," they responded automatically.

Thank god, he thought, reached into his dinner jacket pocket and pulled out a vial of blood.

"It has begun," he announced solemnly. "The time of the Black Sheep in the Wilderness, the Muddy Ram in the Desert, the Great Lord of the Deep Trenches in the Middle of the Pacific, the Dark Four, the Horned Toad, the Coiled Serpent, the Azrabenhorge, the Muzzelothonics, the Whiplakeran, the A'granbxaz, the Old Goat of the Pampas. It has begun."

He held up the vial for all to see and admire.

"And who shall bring the *Bingomomicron* to this august assembly?"

No one answered, which was as it should have been.

"And who shall read the words of the *Bingomomicron* to this august assembly?"

No one answered, which was as it should have been.

"And who shall intone the Final Words of the Final Coming of the Older Deities, culled and studied and learned from the power of the *Bingomomicron?"*

No one answered.

But the light outside had turned a dark green.

✦2✦

The cowled figure pranced joyfully, one might even say drunkenly, in the middle of the deserted street as the night changed color and the crow flew sideways again, looking very bewildered, and the ground trembled ever so slightly, and all the dogs shut up and all the cats shut up and most, but not all, of the lights went out.

Any minute now, he thought ecstatically as he pranced, they'll read the first passage. I'll make my entrance. They'll shit bricks. I'll laugh in their faces. They'll beg for forgiveness. I'll tease them a little. They'll grovel. I'll be strong. They'll offer me their bodies. I'll think about it. They'll offer me their fortunes. I'll snub them. They'll threaten me. I'll laugh in their faces. They'll grovel some more and I'll relent.

Marvelous.

Perfect.

He picked up the hem of his robes, leapt into the air, clicked his sandals together as prescribed by the Parrot Rite of The Coming, and landed with such grace that Ivan Vlaskovich, standing on the curb, applauded.

"Begone!" the cowled figure commanded with a sweep of his commanding arm. He didn't mind the audience, actually, but the adoration could mess up his counting, and counting was the only way he was able to prance with such seeming effortless grace and abandon. One misstep, however, one lost digit, one spin instead of a twirl, and he'd have to start all over again. He didn't want to start all over again. Despite his joy, despite his euphoria, prancing about at night in October was pretty damn boring. Once, he figured, was enough for any man about to become a Younger Deity.

"Scram," he snarled when the little Russian didn't move.

"Just wanted to warn you," Ivan said.

The cowled figure put his hands on his hips and laughed heartily at the sky. "You? Warn me? You?"

Ivan shrugged.

"You? Tell me something I don't already know? You?"

Ivan shrugged again and started to walk away.

"Wait!" the cowled figure commanded.

Ivan stopped and leaned on his ironing board.

"What is it you wanted to warn me about?"

"You said there wasn't anything I could warn you about that you didn't already know."

The cowled figure considered. "True. But it might be amusing to hear what you have to say."

"The crow," the Russian began.

The cowled figure cut him off with a slash of his hand. "I know that one already."

Ivan nodded. "The door—"

"That, too."

Ivan's eyes widened. "You're pretty good."

The cowled figure bowed.

"Your robe's on fire."

The cowled figure laughed mightily as the peasant slouched away into the dark green night, laughed again as he looked up at the spot in the sky where the Older Deities would soon manifest themselves, and laughed when his nostrils wrinkled at the faint stench of smoldering cloth.

"I knew that!" he screamed in the direction the little Russian had taken. Then he ran for his house, and the water spigot on the side. "I knew it, you goddamn peasant! Tonight I know everything!"

The garden hose was still attached. He turned the water on, picked up the hose, and took off his robe, drenched it, soaked it, saturated it, stomped on it just to be sure, then turned the water off and put the robe back on.

"It's a test," he muttered as he realized how heavy saturated wool could get, and how bloody cold. "My faith is being tested."

What he didn't tell the peasant, who was only a peasant after all and not someone you ordinarily confided in, and what he didn't tell the crow that skidded past him sideways with a panicked squawk into the evergreen in the back yard, was that there was, in fact, something he didn't know.

The Russian stepped out from behind the hedge in front of Dr. Smith's house and pointed down toward John Laste's house. "It was them in that black car there that set fire to you. They tried to talk to you but you kept dancing and singing all those weird songs."

"Who are they?" the cowled figure asked, squinting down the street not only at the black car parked in front of the Lastes' house, but also the little red sporty one parked in front of the Putneys' house, and the long blue elegant one just now pulling up in front of the doctor's house.

"I don't know," said the Russian. "I just deliver the warnings. A regular Cassandra, you might say." He sighed and walked away.

"Bastard!" the cowled figure yelled. "You don't even sound like a Russian!" He laughed. He cavorted briefly. Then he raced back to the middle of the street and began his prancing again once he'd brought the count back to mind. It was very intricate, the prancing was, and he couldn't afford to offend the Older Deities by missing a step, or a significant hand movement, or a vital incantation, none of which he had told the others about.

This, then, was his secret.

This was the only way their reading of the sacred *Bingomomicron* was going to bring about their salvation.

He laughed.

He pranced.

He sneezed, blessed himself, and waited impatiently for the sign that the reading had begun.

✦3✦

Kent reached the midway point in the tunnel and paused to rest. Not that the journey thus far had been terribly arduous, and not that he'd had to do battle with hordes and armies of unmentionable creatures ranged against him by whatever hideous alien force Howie the prick had stirred up with his frigging madness; it was the tension that drained him. It happened every time. While he awaited his cue out of camera range on *Passions and Power,* he often felt faint because he had never learned to relax before a performance, or throw up, or any of the other little tricks the big stars claimed they used to prepare themselves for that magical moment under the lights. Which, he supposed, was why he was able to play a butler so well—being tired all the time from nervous exhaustion made him appear as if everything, including his master and mistress, were beneath him even when they weren't shorter.

Now, however, such tricks of the trade would do him no good; now he had to carry on, stiff upper lip, don't disgrace the family, millions of lives depended upon his every step, every breath, every action, every thought.

Jesus, he thought, and damn near fell asleep.

But he moved on.

And thought again that this whole business was entirely too easy.

Did he really expect that Maclemmon would leave that vital to the cause book unguarded in an empty house at the end of a tunnel leading to another empty house?

Did he really believe all he had to do was light a match and that would be that?

"Match?" he said.

His voice echoed.

Water dripped.

Beams and planks creaked.

Things scurried and chittered.

He hurried forward to a place where a great beam braced the ceiling and the walls in such a complicated manner that it made him dizzy to look at it. There, he placed the cleaver on the ground, the gun in his pocket, and frisked himself quite slowly and deliberately. He wanted to make no mistake. He had to be sure.

And when he finished just shy of a strip search, he looked back the way he'd come and said, "Chita, you aren't going to believe this."

He waited then for the miraculous appearance of his partner in saving the world, a caustic quip on her lips, a book of matches in one hand, a bazooka in the other, and a tank strapped to her back. It didn't take much longer than five or ten seconds, however, for him to understand that miracles weren't going to be part of this particular scenario, more's the pity and goddamnit. Which left him with yet another fateful decision to make, and he scowled, spat figuratively, and cursed fluently in four different language groups. He hated decisions; they were too damn decisive for his taste.

As he saw it, he was left with two choices:

First, he could run back to Number 668, scare the hell out of Quentin by bursting out of the refrigerator, run upstairs where he could either waste time rummaging through all the drawers, or simply take the bold route and just ask the guests if anyone had a light. That, of course, entailed some risk, including Quentin over-reacting with the hatchet, or the guests pushing up the timetable for his sacrifice.

Second, he could carry on sans fire-producing material, pray there were no gargoyles or ghouls or eccentric unnatural aberrations guarding the tome, grab the tome, run back to Number 668, dodge Quentin's undoubtedly by now highstrung weapon, run upstairs, and borrow a match.

Third, he could stay where he was until Chita figured out he'd forgotten the matches or thought he was dead and came looking for him. Hopefully, with a match.

Fourth, he could carry on, find the tome and, lacking a proper match or two sticks to rub together, tear it to shreds, flush it down the toilet, and hope that it would serve as a burning because he was being sincere about it.

Fifth, he could give up.

Sixth, he could stand here and yell until Quentin heard him, then yell his problem and hope that Quentin didn't get into another debate with Sheila over who was supposed to stay where during what until which time.

Seventh, he could stop thinking about all the choices he had to choose from, including the two he thought he had had when he had first started, and just do what he always did in situations like this, which was to simply, and with not too much stark naked terror, carry on.

It was a difficult choice.

He wondered what his seldom-mentioned father would do in a sticky situation like this, and decided on a secondary level that since his father had been dead lo these many years, it wouldn't do any good trying to figure it out because being dead took away pretty much all the choices you had to make for the rest of your life.

He carried on.

Everything else carried on, too—the dripping water, the scurrying things, the nearly subliminal subterranean sounds that made tunnel-crawling the exciting sport that it was.

Except, he realized with a perplexed frown, for the light: as he approached the far end after going back to fetch the cleaver, the green glow that had been guiding him toward that far end receded before him, as if, on the one hand, hastily retreating from his determined advance, or, on the other, cleverly luring him toward its source.

When he looked behind him, he could see nothing but black.

It was as if Number 668 simply did not exist.

He wondered if this was one of those the-devil-you-know cases, and decided, as long as he was in the habit, that it didn't make much difference, since devils, strangers or not, were never up to any good.

Whoever thought up that one, he thought, had never met his mother.

He reached his destination not five minutes later, and stood on the threshold of danger and the other basement, scanning the area for possible traps.

What he saw wasn't encouraging.

The other basement was clean. Neat. The floor concrete and painted. The walls covered with a moisture seal painted with murals of a French countryside shortly after the French got it back from the Germans, it didn't make any difference which war, pick one. Squared, painted posts holding up a low ceiling of Italian acoustical tiles. A long workbench with its tools arranged alphabetically and, within the alphabet, in size order. The stairs looked sturdy. He could see, in the shadowed far corner, a modern furnace and water heater gleaming as if they had been just installed.

There were no cobwebs, no neon spiders, no rats, no centipedes, no stench of decay and unearthly body odor.

There was, however, a wishing well in the middle of the floor, with a four-foot brick wall around it.

He stepped into the room cautiously.

Suddenly the peaceful, ordinary, middle-class nature of the entire scene caused alarm bells to go off, and he whirled with an oath, slapped the wall with the flat of the cleaver to silence them, and, simultaneously, turn on a bank of overhead fluorescent lights. They weren't green.

As he passed the staircase, he noticed that the door at the top was barred with thick iron bands upon which had been scratched icons and runes in a foreign, perhaps even alien, language. A mauve waxy substance sealed the rim, and someone had stolen the doorknob.

A trap, something told him.

Well, of course it is, he snapped silently; you don't put something like the *Bingomomicron* in a perfectly ordinary basement without some sort of protective device to either zap the intruder or warn the rightful owner or both, depending upon the nature of the rightful owner, who was, in this instance, dead and therefore undoubtedly capable of practically anything.

A sudden pulse of green from the well startled him.

A glance back at the mouth of the tunnel told him Chita still hadn't bothered to see if he was alive or not.

All right, the way is clear, he told himself; the book must be in the well.

Marvelous, something told him; a way with the incredibly obvious is what you have, don't you?

A talent, he answered; a gift from the gods.

Carefully, he placed the cleaver on one of the steps for easy chopping and swinging access, dropped the gun into his pocket, and approached the well.

A bead of perspiration broke from his temple.

His stomach protested the absence of liquid, and damn strong, fortification.

Every instinct, every sense, every connection with his well-developed, tenacious grip on life told him he was making a huge mistake, that performing this heroic deed would only get him into deeper trouble than he already was in because, in case he hadn't thought about it, which he hadn't, if he did find the *Bingomomicron* in that well, and if he did destroy it and thus stymie the pending return of the Older Deities, there were going to be some very irate acolytes back at the other house who, upon learning that they'd been acolytes for nothing, would probably kill him.

It was something to consider.

The green glow pulsed again.

Wait, he told himself No sense getting up a lather when you don't even know if that book is in there. One step at a time, old man; one step at a time.

He took the step.

With hands braced against the cool brick and a Gaelic prayer at his lips, he leaned over the rim and looked in.

He leaned back.

He dusted his hands.

He rubbed his neck, his chest, the back of his neck.

Shit, he thought.

The book was there.

John Laste, still holding the holy vial of blood, rose from his folding chair. He looked at each of his colleagues in turn, smiling confidently when none looked away but met his gaze calmly and with pride.

"Since I am in possession of the Holy Vial of Blood," he said quietly but with the confident authority of having more money than anyone else in the room, "I shall intone the Final Words of the Final Coming of the Older Deities, so that They shall be pleased with our work, and we shall be rewarded accordingly because They are pleased."

"John," Caroline said in dismay, reminding him of a promise he had made in the heat of such passion as he was able to generate considering his social position, age, and the thought of his wife walking in on his indiscretion.

Marsha's eyes widened. "I knew it," she said. "I knew the cat was dead."

Wally Putney turned to his wife. "Caroline, you don't mean . . . you can't say . . . you haven't . . ." He sputtered. "With him?"

Caroline blushed but held her ground.

"Now wait a minute, hold on there," said Dr. Smith. "You told me you'd get him to let me intone the Final Words of the Final Coming."

"Jesus, Caroline," Wally groaned. "Him, too?"

Smith rolled his eyes. "I wasn't talking to her, you idiot. I was talking to her."

They looked at Pilandra.

She blushed.

Smith leapt to his feet. "Her!" he shouted.

And pointed at Marsha.

John gasped. "Marsha!"

"Marsha?" Caroline queried.

"I promised you nothing," Marsha told the doctor primly. "No more than I promised him."

"Wally?" Caroline queried.

"Wally?" John said.

Wally leapt to his feet. "Now see here," he objected.

They looked.

He blushed.

John demanded an explanation.

Wally whined that it was because of the enormous amount of money he had lent Marsha several years ago, for the shoring up of the Laste Roundup chain of sauteed barbecue restaurants famed throughout New England and parts of Minnesota for their hot sauce and cross buns.

"Marsha, is this true?"

"Without it," she confessed proudly, "we would have gone broke."

"But we were doing so well, all those grand openings, all those checks. How could we possibly go broke?"

"Because of the embezzlement."

Caroline crossed her legs in utter confusion.

"I have never touched a penny except for personal and business reasons," he defended himself stoutly.

"Not yours," she said. "Mine."

"Yours?"

Dr. Smith wanted to know why he wasn't going to get to say the Final Words of the Final Coming.

Pilandra put a hand on his knee to calm him, and Rex shook his head in subtle warning, lest someone notice the act of familiarity.

Meanwhile, John began to nod. "I see. So you borrowed an obscene amount of money from Wally Putney to cover the fact that you had embezzled all that money from the Roundup."

"No," she said. "To pay the blackmail."

"Oh my god," Wally whispered.

John continued to nod. "I see. You were being blackmailed because someone had discovered your acts of embezzlement, which, by the way, dear, means you're fired, you realize that, don't you?"

"No," she said. "Because of . . ." Suddenly Marsha burst into tears. Instantly, Rex knelt before her, a handkerchief in his hand. She smiled bravely and dried her tears. "Thank you," she said gratefully.

"Think nothing of it," he said, stood, faced the room, and whipped off his patch.

"My god!" John gasped. "It's you!"

"You!" Wally stammered.

"You!" Caroline blushed.

"You?" Kenilworth queried. He frowned at John. "I think, under the circumstances, John, I should be the one to say the Final Words of the Final Coming."

Defeated and crushed, John folded back into his chair, thrashed around until Rex extricated him, and sat on the hearth, head down. "Under the circumstances, Kenilworth, I believe you're right."

Caroline pouted.

Marsha said, "In a pig's eye. It's my turn, you old fart."

"Now wait a minute," Wally protested. "Despite this unsettling turn of events, I do think I'm next in line, don't you think?"

"No," said Rex Regal, so firmly, so forcefully, so loudly, that everyone stopped gaping and staring and gasping, and looked at him in fear and awe. Even John, crushed by the traffic on the road of life as he was, lifted his head.

"We do not have time for this petty nonsense," Rex declared with a winsome smile.

"I hardly think embezzlement and impending poverty is petty," Marsha complained, although she put a pleasant spin on it so not to offend him.

"What blackmail?" John asked.

"In the scheme of things, my dear," Rex said so gently that she blushed half her wrinkles into oblivion, "I think everything is petty just about now, don't you agree?" He pointed to the dark green night. "The Older Deities are nearly upon us. Our differences, as petty as they may be, must be postponed for the greater good. I don't think They would be pleased if They arrived in the middle of a family squabble."

Marsha and Caroline instantly nodded at the wisdom of the pronouncement; Wally, his limpid hair all limp and his watery eyes sparkling with renewed purpose, shrugged, although he did pat his wife's shoulder in a gesture of solidarity and temporary forgiveness; and Pilandra beamed proudly.

Only Dr. Smith refused to join the circle of dedicated acolyte-bonding; instead, he dragged his black bag onto his lap and opened it.

Rex moved to the center of the room. He held out his hand. "John?"

A brief moment of hesitation marked the passing of the mantle before John handed over the Holy Vial of Blood.

And immediately it fell within Rex's grasp, the blood began to glow.

"All we need now," he said with a charmingly evil smile, "is the *Bingomomicron,* and all our troubles will be over."

Inside the well was a darkstone pillar that rose to within three feet of the rim. On the darkstone pillar, which turned slowly counterclockwise by a devious mechanism that appeared to be anchored at the very center of the Earth, was a somewhat smaller, crude lightstone altar; on the lightstone altar, which had an inordinate amount of bloodstains soaked into it, was a sturdy gold and copper bookstand inscribed with runes and alien characters of an indescribable nature.

On the bookstand was the *Bingomomicron.*

It was exactly as Chita had described it back when she was Hester; it was also a lot uglier. Nothing exquisite here, nor even so awful that it took on a perverse beauty. It was just plain ugly, no getting around it, and he hoped that it had not been made in the Older Deities' image; if it had been, they wouldn't have to lift a claw against the opposition since the opposition would simply wither away from the massive shock to its collective aesthetic sensibilities.

Then, as he struggled to keep his gorge from rising, he noticed that far below the stone altar was a grid of thick bars blocking the throat of the well. He also noticed, since his curiosity hadn't been warned to knock it off, that the grid was several levels deep. How deep he could not tell. How far each level was from the other he could not tell. How thick the grid bars were he could not tell, but they were pretty thick.

He wondered about it.

He stopped wondering about it when it occurred to him that the grid definitely hadn't been placed there to keep the book from tumbling to the center of the Earth should it fall from its stone altar.

"Damn," he said.

But there was no time for further introspection, speculation, or rationalization. He could see another pulse of green working its way toward him from the depths of the well. He had to work, and work fast. Time was of the essence.

So, with a deep breath, he leaned over the rim and reached in.

In the middle of the street, the cowled figure stopped dancing and stared expectantly at Number 668.

• • •

In the kitchen at Number 668, Chita and Sheila stood at the sink, wondering what in hell they were going to feed all those people since no one had told them that the stove was gas, and the gas had been turned off. Yet, from the raised and angry voices in the back parlor, they also realized that the guests probably weren't too hungry anyway and that the dinner had probably only been a ruse to get them into the house so that they could perform their obscene rituals without anyone except those already in the house becoming suspicious.

Chita drummed her fingers thoughtfully on the sink's chipped rim.

Sheila tapped her foot impatiently on the chipped linoleum floor.

Finally Chita said, "I've got to get Kent."

Sheila was aghast. "But you can't."

"I have to," she answered. "He comes back here with that book, those people are going to murder him."

"But he's supposed to burn it."

Chita smiled at the foolishness of the young. "Matches," she said wisely. "He don't got no stinking matches."

"He don't? But that's terrible."

"Lords are like that," Chita educated her as she turned the young woman toward the dining room and gave her a gentle shove. "They got all these people to do their thinking for them, so when they have to think for themselves they go a little crazy sometimes. Trust me. He forgot the matches."

Sheila turned with a frown. "Quentin isn't supposed to let anybody down there."

"Neither are you."

"I forgot." She took a step back into the room.

Chita smiled, much as Rex had smiled at the gathering in the back parlor, the evilly charming one. The smile, not the parlor.

Sheila, being young but not stupid, stopped.

The voices also stopped, then started again, this time replacing their arguments, accusations, and heated denials with a monotonic monotonous chant accompanied by someone beating time on the seat of a chair. Sheila's eyes widened in horror and she looked to Chita for guidance.

Chita, who had recovered her butcher knife, told her to see what they were doing.

"They're chanting."

Chita then suggested that the young woman insinuate herself into the dining room, position herself beside the doorway to the back parlor, and make sure that the acolytes didn't leave the room. If they needed help chanting, Sheila was to help them; if they needed help remembering the words, Sheila was to make them up; if they tried to leave, Sheila was to use whatever force and power within her disposal to keep them here.

"That's what the baron told me, too. But he didn't tell me what to do if they hit me or anything."

"Fake it," Chita said.

Sheila's eyes widened again, this time in admiration. "You know, that's what Quentin always tells me. It has something to do with the male ego. Do you think—"

But Chita was already gone, the basement door practically ripped off in her hands as she flung it open, flung herself down the steps, dodged Quentin's belated hatchet, and plunged without thought to personal safety into the refrigerator.

It wasn't until she was halfway there that she realized she'd forgotten the matches.

Sheila, true to her word and used to obeying unreasonable demands, sensuously insinuated herself into the dining room, unobtrusively positioned herself by the entrance to the back parlor, and was about to set in motion a nebulous plan to prevent the acolytes from leaving the room when, without warning and suddenly, Rex stood before her.

"My god," she said, "it's you!"

Someone tapped her on the shoulder. She spun around away from Rex into the surprised but not unwilling arms of Quentin Eddye, who looked over her shoulder and said, "Hi, Pop."

Trying to ignore the green glow racing toward the outside world as opposed to the murky and mysterious depths of the Earth, Kent picked the book off the bookstand.

Chita considered half a dozen choices.

Sheila, and everyone else in the back parlor except Pilandra who already knew, said, "Pop?"

• • •

Kent frowned as he backed away from the well and dropped to the floor just as the green glow exploded into the air, splashed against the ceiling, and faded.

Rex? he thought.

Chita burst into the exceptionally neat and clean basement, saw Kent rising shakily from the floor with a really humongous book in his hands, and shouted, "I forgot the frigging matches!"

Kent looked at the book.

Chita looked at the book. "God," she said in a non-blasphemous expression of utter distaste.

He placed the book on the floor, wiped his hands on his jeans, and pulled out his gun. "Maybe," he said, "I could shoot it."

"Maybe," she answered, "you could shoot that," and she pointed at the well, from the depths of which came a grumbling and muffled roaring that had, they knew instinctively, nothing to do with another arrival of the green glow.

And it was then that Kent realized that Howmaster Maclemmon, con man, thief, and fairly decent amateur astronomer, had tricked them all.

The trouble was, he didn't know whether there was any time left to do anything about it.

•4•

In the best of all possible worlds, none of which Kent seemed to live in or was destined for, there would be a crate of fresh dynamite tucked under the workbench, complete with caps, plunger, and wire, the assembly of which would permit him to destroy the house, seal the well and tunnel with flaming debris, and forever, or at least for the next hundred years or so, protect the world from the proverbial fate worse than death; in the best of all possible worlds, he would be able to flip open the vile book, run his finger swiftly down the table of contents, find the spell or the directions or the instructions to send the Older Deities back where they came from, and give the world a chance to figure out how to deal with them the next time they decided to come home; in the absolute best of all possible worlds, however, he wouldn't be in this mess to begin with.

Another, more intense pulse of green briefly illuminated the lighted basement.

"So," said Chita as she backed nervously toward the tunnel entrance, "what are you going to do?"

Kent gathered up the book, and the cleaver, and shook his head. "I don't know."

"You don't have a plan?"

"No."

"You came all the way over here without a plan?"

He gave her a look she didn't want, so gave it back with one of her own. "When I came over here," he reminded her sourly, "the plan was to burn this damn thing. I don't have any matches. I waited for you to bring the matches. You came, but you don't have any matches. There's no dynamite, no acetylene torch, no flares, no firecrackers, no belching dragon. The best thing I reckon we can do is return to the house and see if any of them know what to do with it."

She stared at him.

He shrugged. "Okay, so they know what to do with it. Maybe I can bargain with them."

"What for?"

"To stall, darlin'," he said. "To stall. Long enough, if I'm lucky, to figure something out."

Without waiting for a response, which he didn't want to hear anyway because he had guessed what it would be, he hurried into the tunnel as the house began to vibrate a little, and the tools on the workbench began to sway to the gentle rhythm of impending doom.

Another pulse of green followed hard behind, forcing them to notice that the pulses were coming more rapidly, closer together, and more intensely, which was, for the pulses as they'd studied them in the limited time available, natural.

"They won't bargain, you know," Chita pointed out, keeping so close to him that he could feel her soft hot breath on the back of his neck which, under different circumstances, would have added a dash of Latin spice to the adventure; as it was, it only made him sweat.

"If I threaten to tear it up in front of their eyes so they can't use whatever it is they need to do for whatever it is they need to do, they'll bargain."

"Last count," she said, "there were seven of them and four of us, if you count the girl and her boyfriend."

The rumbling through the tunnel returned, this time more violently. Subsequently it was difficult to keep their feet, and the roof and pieces of supporting plank and beam began to fall in a shower of dust and parts of the roof and some of the supporting planks and beams. Chita fell once in the race toward safety and cried out; Kent turned at the unexpected, and potent, obscenity, saw her vanishing in the swirl of tunnel debris, and grabbed her hand, yanked her free and to her feet, and embraced her quickly before moving on. When she tripped a second time over a pile of animal bones, he again returned her to her feet and embraced her quickly to reassure her that they would, given luck and a shorter tunnel, make it back to the house alive. When she tripped a third time, he stared at her.

"Hey," she said, scrambling to her feet on her own, "you gotta take moments of personal comfort when you can, you know what I mean?"

They ran on.

Although the growling and the rumbling from the well was no longer audible, Kent figured it was because the rumbling in the tunnel was growing steadily louder. At the same time, and distressingly so, stones and pebbles falling from the walls and roof were replaced by rocks and boulders; the puddles slipped noisily through widening cracks that began to appear in the floor; the overhead beams used to hold up the roof were losing their grip with a lot of moaning and groaning; and not a single thing scurried from shadow to shadow.

Kent shifted the notorious *Bingomomicron* to carry it under his left arm, then reached out and grabbed Chita with his free hand.

They ran on.

A distant explosion behind them sent a tidal wave, or a fairly large cloud, or a steamy breath, of madly swirling dust after them. They were soon enveloped in the wave, cloud, or steamy breath and were effectively rendered blind. In such a manner then did they continue to run, not worrying about where the walls were because they found them fairly well without half trying; also the moaning supporting beams, some good-size rocks, and a boulder that had worked its way out of the wall and partially blocked their escape until Kent used his nearly superhuman strength born of desperation to get the hell out of here in one piece to squeeze past it and pull Chita safely after him.

They ran on, but he didn't think they were going to make it.

They made it.

They stumbled into the ratty, disgusting, half-rotten basement of Number 668, fell gratefully to their knees and coughed, retched, coughed, choked, gagged, and wiped their eyes with the backs of whatever hands they happened to have open at the time.

Though most of the dust didn't follow, the rumbling, and some of the vibrating, did.

As they recovered, he noticed that, as Chita helped him to his feet, she made every attempt not to touch the *Bingomomicron,* and he didn't blame her. It wasn't covered with slime, but it felt like it; it wasn't coated with poison, but it felt like it; it wasn't dripping blood or acid or ichor or intestinal remnants, but it felt like it.

Jesus, he thought, and threw it on the floor.

The rumbling stopped.

The vibrations eased.

Dust clung to the air like a funereal fog.

"Are you all right?" he asked.

Chita shook her ruffles. "I'm never gonna get this thing clean."

She was all right.

So he cast the cleaver aside, glanced at the refrigerator, and picked the book up gingerly, nodded to the stairs, stared when she shook her head in an emphatic *no way in hell* fashion, nodded more forcefully, and started up without waiting for another objection; he had, after all, plenty of objections of his own, and no one had listened to him, so why should he listen to her.

As he climbed, he realized that he still had no idea what he was going to do once he got into the kitchen, but he hoped that something would come to him. Not that it usually did in situations like this. Usually he was at a loss until something came to him, and sometimes something came just a beat too late for it to do him any good. Usually it was damn clever, too, which was a shame.

It wasn't until he had reached the top step that the distant echoes of the rumbling in the collapsing tunnel faded completely and he could hear the replacement rumbling of many voices; it wasn't until he was in the kitchen, blinking in the bright light of the tomato-shaped chandelier, that he realized the replacement rumbling was chanting.

"Damn," he said in a lowered voice as Chita joined him, still shaking her ruffles and leaving rocks behind, "it's already started."

The chanting stopped.

Kent frowned.

Then he heard someone say, "Hi, Pop," and looked at Chita for an explanation.

She shrugged.

He started for the dining room, stopped, opened a random cupboard door and shoved the book inside, closed the door, and started for the dining room. There, standing in the entrance to the back parlor, were Quentin and Sheila.

And: "Son of a bitch," he said. "Rex."

Rex Regal looked over the heads of the embracing young couple and said, "Goddamn. Kent."

"So," Kent said. "Rex."

"Ah," said Rex. "Kent."

"Hey," said Chita. "What?"

For an answer, and one he thought was pretty good all things considered, he pulled out his gun.

Immediately, Quentin protested the unwarranted show of force, although he had sense enough to pull Sheila out of the way as Kent moved forward, backing a wryly smiling Rex into the other room where the others fell instantly silent when Rex backed in, smiling wryly, and Kent came in frontward, and Chita came in behind them with a butcher knife in her hand.

"What is the meaning of this intrusion?" John Laste demanded haughtily.

Kent leaned deceptively casually against the jamb and used the gun to wave Rex across the room until he had seated himself beside Pilandra Eddye. The man never once exhibited a trace of nervousness, nor did he betray any thought of attempting to disarm Kent, or escape, for which Kent was grateful since he'd just remembered that, having forgotten the matches, he'd also forgotten if he'd remembered to load the gun after he'd taken it out of his suitcase up in his bedroom without the bed.

Bluffing, however, was an integral part of a baron's upbringing, especially when Nanny was showing four cards to a straight flush, ace high.

He allowed himself the temporary luxury of a one-sided, brief smile. "So," he said to the room at large. "You're the ones who want to sacrifice me tonight."

"Ah," said John carefully when recognition arrived a skipped heartbeat later. "It's you, is it?"

Kent nodded.

The others murmured.

"How . . . how did you know about the you know what?" Wally asked timidly. He cleared his throat loudly. "And how dare you assume that we are involved."

To which Kent replied, "Bugger off."

"Well!"

"Exactly."

Idly, lips pursed in a silent moist whistle, Chita began to clean her fingernails with the butcher knife; a nice touch, Kent thought, since it kept the others watching her instead of him, unless it had something to do with the fact that some of her ruffles had fallen off. What he was going to do about it was another question entirely.

He decided to go for it, what the hell: "Anybody got a match?"

Caroline immediately plucked her spangled purse from the floor and began to sift through it. Wally gaped, slapped the purse from her hands, and indicated without a word why Kent wanted the combustible device. When she understood, she turned angrily and said, "Baron!"

He shrugged; nothing ventured, nothing gained, you're not as stupid as you look even if Marsha over there had made a move toward her own purse.

"It doesn't make any difference, actually, does it?" he said. "I have the *Bingomomicron,* and you don't. I have the only means by which you can make that final call to the Older Deities, and you don't. I have what you require for your grotesque plan to succeed, and you don't." His smile, though not charmingly evil, was baronial enough to make most of them shiver; all, in fact, except Rex, who merely shifted uncomfortably.

John Laste paled and sputtered. "But . . . but you must let us have it, Baron. You must. You don't know what you're dealing with here."

Kent pushed away from the jamb and glared at him. "My friend, I know more than you think."

"Then you know we will *all* die unless you give me that book without another second's delay."

"John," he answered calmly, "if I'm going to die, I'm not going to be the only one."

"Hey," Chita said.

Behind him, Sheila sobbed and broke from Quentin's embrace.

"You know nothing," sneered Dr. Smith.

Kent sighed and shook his head.

"Hey, Lord, can I sit down?" Chita asked when she saw him take a breath.

He looked at her, affronted that she would imply a need to rest her legs because he was about to become long-winded.

She reminded him with an impatient sweep of the knife that long-winded would get them killed since those guys in the well weren't going to wait for lengthy expositions, this being real life and all.

He nodded at the point well taken and would she mind aiming it elsewhere.

Chita stuck the knife into the wall.

He turned to the others, cleared his throat, ignored Chita's groan, and said:

"You all know, of course, that Rex here is, in reality, Quentin's father, the result of a short but significant liaison between himself and Pilandra Eddye just before her husband drowned heroically in that tragic accident at the ice cream factory some twenty-some years ago. Naturally she never told anyone who the real father was, not even her husband, who was dead. Just as she never told Wally there that her brief but inconsequential liaison with him had been keenly observed by Dr. Smith there, who was blackmailing Marsha there into financing his orchestrated experiments in genetic engineering being conducted in the basement laboratory under his office. What Dr. Smith didn't know, of course, is that Caroline, as a result of her concurrent liaison with him, knew all about it and threatened to expose him with his clothes on if he didn't convince Wally that she could not bear children, since she didn't want to have to buy all new clothes since Wally's business had been ruined by his ex-wife, which is why he killed her."

He paused dramatically then for an assortment of gasps and feeble denials.

"Meanwhile, Caroline and Rex were messing around in a fairly platonic way so that Rex could gain entrance to Langford Place society in order to keep an eye on his growing son, who he didn't know he had until he heard about it from Amy, the busybody hippo in the Gutted Oyster. What he didn't know, however, was that John over there had messed around with Caroline over here just long enough for Caroline to become utterly dependent upon his erotic ministrations so that he could, eventually, blackmail Wally about the ex-wife's murder and not worry about Caroline screwing things up because he was blackmailing her too. Wally, unbeknownst to John, however, was already plotting with Kenilworth to drive John out of town because John had had a liaison with Caroline, Marsha had slipped on the odd mattress with Wally and Kenilworth, and Pilandra had it all on video tape thanks to the electronic genius of her son, who took after his father, even though he didn't know that his real father wasn't dead until tonight, when he, being a well-trained observant actor, recognized the telltale Eddye hair."

One of the women fainted noisily, unless it was Wally.

"However," Kent continued grimly, "what none of you really knew was that Hester Kerwin was in reality Chita Juarel, who was never Howmaster's mistress at all, but a spy hired *by me* to make sure that Howmaster never bothered me again. When she learned of the diabolical plan you had planned, however, she made sure Maclemmon's will was altered so that I would become the sole heir, come to Hamtucket, and expose you all.

"Yes, my astonished, bug-eyed friends, it was Chita who called you all tonight in order to upset your equilibria and fuzzy your thinking processes. It was she who pretended to be Lorenzo Jones, Dr. Smith's former partner squeezed out of the genetic proceeds by his allergies to Petrie dishes; it was she who pretended to be the dead ex-wife of Wally Putney; and through the miracle of her home English language and dialect mimicking course, it was indeed she who pretended to be the disowned disenchanted children of John and Marsha returned to take rightful possession of their possessions."

Then he laughed at their consternation.

"Yes," he said. "While you were all plotting and scheming and planning and sneaking about, I knew all along what was going on." He snapped his fingers. "And now I shall take care of the *Bingomomicron* and end this farce forever."

• • •

A fraction of a second passed while the threat made the rounds.

Then: "The hell you will," said Wally Putney as he leapt boldly to his feet and pulled out his weapon.

"Damn right," John agreed, leaping to his feet and pulling out his weapon.

"All for one, damnit," Smith concurred eagerly, leaping to his feet, grabbing his black bag, opening it, and pulling out his weapon.

Marsha reached into her demure neckline, pulled out her weapon, but didn't bother to leap to her feet; all this talk had exhausted her emotionally.

Pilandra didn't move.

And Rex didn't leap to his feet or pull out his weapon, but he did cross his legs and dare Kent with a disdainful look to try to shoot them all before the Older Deities showed up and finished the job for him.

Kent, sneering at Rex for his blond naivete, mentioned in the faces of danger and all those pointing weapons that Maclemmon was neither their protector nor their benefactor, as they had formally believed. Being true to his nature, he had *tricked them all* into believing that the Older Deities *really needed* their ceremonial supplications to find out where to land, when, in fact, *they were already here!* at this very moment *climbing out of a well!* in the house *next door!* and he didn't think they gave a damn one way or the other who was waiting for them.

"Because, you see," he concluded ominously, "when they get here, you pitiful sods, they're going to be . . . hungry."

No one spoke.

"I don't believe it," John said at last.

"Which part?"

"Howmaster's not really needing us, of course."

"Why, John!" Marsha exclaimed.

"Well, that part too, my dear. It goes without saying."

"It already did," she said, and shot him.

John gaped at the shallow but agonizing crease that neatly traversed his evening trouser leg and fell back onto his chair, which collapsed. He had no opportunity to complain, however, because Caroline, miffed at his refusal to deny their personal relationship, creased his other leg just before Wally creased his left arm, sending his personally made .357 derringer skittering across the floor to Rex's feet. Rex instantly picked the gun up and aimed it at Kent, but was distracted when Dr. Smith creased Wally's right arm, Caroline creased Smith in the left thigh, Marsha, who was getting pretty good, creased Caroline just at the hemline, and John, gasping but cleverly using his one good hand, winged his wife, Caroline, Wally, and just missed taking off Kenilworth's left ear.

It all happened so fast that Kent didn't have a chance to move.

Chita, on the other hand, darted into the dining room, grabbed the back of his sweater and yanked him safely out of the way.

"You know," she told him, as the firing continued sporadically in the next room, "I didn't do none of that stuff like you said I did."

"I know."

"You know? Then how did you know all that other stuff?"

"I didn't."

"You didn't?"

He shook his head. "But I always wanted to say lines like that. The butler never said lines like that. I got to comment on the weather once in a while, but that was about it." He grinned. "God, it felt good."

"I'm happy for you," Chita said crabbily.

"Excuse me, but someone's at the door," Quentin interrupted nervously.

"Don't answer it," Kent ordered.

"Why?"

"Because," he answered grimly, "I know who it is."

"Oh, go on." Quentin laughed. "You can't know. It's impossible."

"Trust me," Kent said flatly. "I know."

The house took to vibrating again, not quite as gently as it had done earlier.

The chandeliers swayed.

Things rattled softly in the kitchen.

Shots were fired in the back parlor, but since they were without the accompaniment of death-screams and the thud of falling bodies, Kent reckoned they were still wounding and creasing and winging and scratching each other all to hell. Another mental calculation suggested that he had about five minutes before they ran out of ammunition, moaned a lot, checked the flow of blood, and finally realized that he, their sacrifice, wasn't in there anymore.

Rex came to the doorway.

Kent looked at him.

Rex pointed the derringer at Kent's forehead and pulled the trigger.

The hammer, in the horrified silence that followed the pulling of the trigger, came down on an empty chamber.

Kent slugged him.

Rex staggered backward into the room where he was inadvertently winged by Pilandra, who had snatched Marsha's gun from her hand and was trying to plug Dr. Smith, who was trying to bandage as many parts of himself as he could reach while dodging Wally's bullets and Caroline's contemptuous glances.

Kent blew on his hand to alleviate the pain flaring across his knuckles, and was about to follow up on his advantage when a blur crossed his vision.

"Jesus!" he yelled when he realized what it was. "Stop that woman!"

But it was too late.

Sheila opened the door.

"What?" she demanded, all decorum fled in the face of all the shooting and slugging and winging and bleeding.

A cowled figure stood on the porch. There was a large gun in its pudgy right hand. The gun pointed at Sheila's breast, which heaved at the sight and pushed the rest of her back into the house. The cowled figure grabbed her arm, put the gun to her temple, and grinned.

"Well, well, well," it said. "Looks like you almost made it, Kent boy."

"And the horse you rode in on, Howie," Kent said.

The dialogue had taken place during a lull in the shooting and bandaging, and so Kent wasn't surprised at the gasps and cries of astonishment from the back parlor, at the crowd that suddenly crowded into the dining room, or at the way Chita cleverly yanked the butcher knife from its place in the wall and slipped it under her shirt.

"Howie?" said John.

"Howie?" said Caroline.

"Oh, give it a rest," said Kent wearily. "We all know it's Howmaster Maclemmon, recently returned from the land of the dead, here to make sure that his plans don't get screwed up."

"Very nice, Kent," Maclemmon admitted. He tossed back the cowl. It was, not surprisingly, the pudgy face from the mummy case in the attic. Except that the brown eyes were a little closer together, and he needed a shave. Maclemmon, not the mummy case. "Very nice indeed. But I've been listening outside the back parlor window, and I'm sorry to say you're wrong about one thing."

"And what's that?" he asked, although he knew damn well what it was, but it was expected of him.

"The sacrifice," Maclemmon answered.

John grabbed Kent's arm as best he could, what with all the bullet creases and bandages on his arms and all. "Right here, O Master."

"Wrong," Maclemmon chortled. "He's not the sacrifice. *You* are."

"Me?"

"Not just you, you dolt. All of you."

"Us?" was the unison chorus of amazement and betrayal.

Maclemmon laughed evilly, cut himself off abruptly, and ordered everyone into the back parlor.

"The time has come," the madman said. "You've had your fun. Now you're all going to . . . *die*."

– VIII –

The Edge of Night

✦1✦

Once upon a time, many years ago, Kent decided to leave his semi-isolated Hebrides isle estate to explore the wide world beyond the watery horizon. After bribing the servants to keep their mouths shut, and making sure all his mother's armored motorcraft were disabled, as well as the gunship helicopter and the hovercraft, he said farewell to the wenches, and the twins in the village, and rowed at midnight into the blunted teeth of a mild autumn storm with nothing but the clothes on his back and a few thousand pounds in his pocket. Once he reached the mainland, he climbed every mountain, forded every stream, and hiked through tons of cowshit until he found his dream—an empty manger on a deserted croft with running water. There, he washed, slept until dawn, and made his way to the nearest village from which he traveled by rail to Edinburgh, and thence to Birmingham, Merkleton, Coventry, and finally, London. He was dry by that time, and fellow passengers no longer winced or gagged or turned politely away from the pungent aroma of damp but tailored wool. His next stop was a hotel not far from the British Museum; the stop after that was a pub where he managed, after several tries, to locate and identify his liquor limit.

A month or so later, he ran across Howmaster Maclemmon in Bloomsbury Park, picked him up, shared a meal and old times, and was almost immediately bilked out of the rest of his pocket money. Luckily, Kent was no longer the simple country baron out to be fleeced in the big bad city; luckily, he had made a few wise investments in haggis futures; luckily, he had ascertained through the helpful greed of one of his family's legal retainers not only the alarming extent of his mother's network of paid Highland assassins, but also knowledge of a battle guru in Brixton who himself had extensive knowledge of fisticuffs, an ancient and currently outmoded form of aggressive communication.

Maclemmon had bilked him; Kent tracked him down and beat him senseless.

It wouldn't be the last time.

So it was that when Maclemmon snarled the cowering dedicated acolytes back into the back parlor, Kent, using the subtle breathing and retreat techniques taught to him by the wizened Brixton Buddha, cleverly stepped noiselessly to one side of the doorway into the dining room and waited for Howie to come through with his whimpering hostage. Maclemmon, for all that he was consummate in a lot of things like bilking, was also about as stupid as a lemming with a road map.

As expected, Sheila came through first, copious tears streaking her saintly cheeks, her hair all mussed from the tussle in the hall.

Maclemmon followed fairly immediately, his weapon poking at the small of her back, his feet shuffling to prevent his tripping over his hem.

Chita, who had also cleverly retreated herself into the kitchen, whistled once to get his attention, and brandished her butcher knife.

Maclemmon looked up and glared. "In here, tramp," he said disgustedly. "I can shoot faster than you can throw."

"Tramp?" she said.

Maclemmon sneered.

Kent, meanwhile, wasted no time. He chopped with his right hand, thus disabling Maclemmon's gun hand; swung with his left hand, thus disabling Maclemmon's jaw; and lashed out with his right foot, thus disabling Maclemmon.

Chita cheered alliteratively.

At the same time, Kent grabbed Sheila's arm and spun her effortlessly toward the kitchen while, at approximately the same time, he grabbed Maclemmon's gun from the floor, kicked Maclemmon several times rather smartly in the slats, and noticed that those previously cowering in the back parlor had overcome their fear and sense of betrayal and were pooling ammunition for their arsenal, some of which was already aimed in his direction.

He ran.

Shots were fired.

The house continued to tremble.

The chandelier in the front parlor broke loose from its plaster mooring and crashed to the floor in an impressive shower of sparks and hissing wires.

Chita threw open the busted door to the filthy mud porch, shoved Sheila through, stepped aside to let Quentin run through, then gestured for Kent to hurry up, they didn't have all night and neither did the world, in case he was interested.

Kent understood.

The chandelier in the upper hallway swayed and fell and shattered on the floor, impressively.

Shots were fired.

Kent whirled and fired a few wild shots of his own, mostly of a warning nature, which sent Caroline shrieking madly back into the back parlor, Dr. Smith scurrying into the front parlor from the front hall, Wally leaping nimbly out of sight into the dining room, and John ducking back into the back parlor where he collided with his wife, who winged him stingingly across the right knee. Accidentally, this time; they had already buried the hatchet in the baseboard.

Once outside, Kent and the others pressed themselves against the outer wall beside the outside steps to the filthy mud porch to formulate their next move. Naturally it would involve a lot of running and ducking and dodging and diving, but it was the direction they lacked. If they ran around the house, surely someone would spot them from a window, alert the others, and they'd all or most of them be cut down before they reached the perceived safety of the street; if they tried to scale the high stockade fence at the back of the yard, no doubt someone would spot them from a window and pick them off one by one before a single leg was thrown over to pull them to the safety of the next block; if they ran into the garage, they'd be trapped whether anyone spotted them from a window or not; if they tried to make it next door and alert the hithertofore unmentioned neighbors, they ran the risk that no one would be home, thus trapping them like mad dogs.

They could also run over there to the house under which was the well from which Kent had pulled the *Bingomomicron.*

"Oh shit."

Chita looked at Sheila. "What did I tell you?"

"It's all right," Quentin said calmly, finally relinquishing his ax for one of Kent's smoking revolvers. "Don't worry, I have a plan."

Kent was skeptical.

"It's easy, we just take a hostage," the young man told them. "Then we force them back into the house, to the front, see, and then we can grab the book from wherever the baron put it, and get out before they can stop us. See, as long as we have the hostage like a shield like, they won't dare shoot for fear of killing one of their own."

"They seemed to be doing okay before," Chita told him.

"But that was before Maclemmon was there to unite them."

"He wants to kill them all, remember? He told them that."

Quentin frowned.

"Besides," Kent added, "they're not going to be that stupid, running out here without checking first to be sure we're harmless."

The porch door slammed outward, fell off one hinge, and Caroline tripped delightfully down the steps in her sultry high heels, a matching semiautomatic in her hands, which were gloved to avoid the grease.

I am forever amazed, Kent thought.

He glanced skyward—and grateful, of course, it goes without saying.

He stepped out of the shadows he'd forgotten he was in, snatched the gun away, and grabbed Caroline snugly around the waist.

"Oh, Baron," she gasped, wide-eyed and panting as she clamped herself submissively to his aristocratic form.

"You'll never know," he told her regretfully, and marched her back into the house where everyone else had gathered in the kitchen. When they saw the odd procession come in from the filthy mud porch, they backed hastily back into the dining room, where Maclemmon still lay on the floor, holding various parts of his injured body, but mostly his slats.

Kent said not a word.

Caroline wriggled furiously in an attempt to get away, or something.

Kent said not a word. He couldn't; if he tried, he'd squeak.

"You won't get away with this, you foreign fool," said John Laste stiffly. "The only way you can save yourself is by giving yourself up and letting us sacrifice you."

"That's correct, medically speaking," agreed Dr. Smith. He knelt beside Maclemmon.

"Isn't that correct, Howmaster?"

Maclemmon, who had managed a sitting position, could only gasp and nod and glare at Kent.

"And if I don't?" Kent asked ingenuously.

"But . . ." John looked around him. "My god, man, think of the women!"

Kent looked at Marsha, at Caroline, at Pilandra Eddye. His eyes widened in startled, belated, but timely recognition.

And Pilandra, who had been trying desperately to remain part of the group experience and still hide behind Rex, shook her head as if to warn him not to tell them what he knew.

Kent grinned. "Well, well, well." He tightened his grip on Caroline, who was by now close to swooning, and panting hard enough to create a breeze.

"Don't," Pilandra ordered harshly when he opened his mouth. She stepped away from Rex, who looked at her, puzzled, and then at the gun she pointed at Kent. "One word, and I'll shoot."

"You'll hit Caroline," Kent told her, making sure Caroline was in a position to make him truthful for a change.

"I could care," she sneered.

"Thank god," Wally breathed.

Pilandra pulled the hammer back. "Let her go."

"If I let her go," Kent said reasonably, "you'll shoot me to keep me from telling what I know. If I don't let her go, you'll shoot her and the bullet will no doubt and with my luck pass right through her meaty parts and kill me. If I call your bluff, you'll shoot. If I shoot first, you'll shoot anyway . . ."

He took a deep breath.

"Sunday."

Pilandra gasped at the verbal blow, so surprised she forgot to pull the trigger. The others gasped, so surprised they forgot to ask what the hell was going on. "Sunday?" Wally said.

"Sunday?" John queried.

"This little gal here?" Dr. Smith wondered aloud. "Our gal?" Marsha wanted to know.

"Sunday?" Rex said, aghast.

"Indeed it is that very same," Kent answered knowledgeably. He reached up and opened a cupboard. "The very same Sunday Eddye who vanished from sight about twenty years ago in California, London, and all the fashionable capitals of the world. A sharp little girl, the last I heard." He grinned. He opened another cupboard. "Tell me, love, can a little girl from a mining town in the West really find happiness married to a wealthy and titled Englishman, hmmmm?"

"Fuckin' A," she snarled. "But it's better when he's dead."

Another round of gasps, including one from the robed Maclemmon, who, with Smith's awkward assistance, struggled to his feet and slapped at his robe to get it to fall right. "Damn you, Kent," he said.

Kent kept grinning, and opened another cupboard. Caroline, by this time, was beyond hope and into fantasy.

"It appears to me," Rex said thoughtfully, "that we have a Mexican standoff here, don't you think, Kent old man?"

"Dry up, big boy," Sunday, aka Pilandra, Eddye snarled. "There's no effing standoff when we have more guns and bullets than the stupid *actor* does."

Rex nodded the point.

Kent opened another cupboard, doing his best to disguise his clandestine activity as a way of preventing Caroline from slumping moaning to the floor, and simultaneously using his features to speak volumes about the sneering, caustic way Sunday had spoken the title of his profession. But she always had been openly contemptuous of those with artistic skills, he remembered; even as an orphaned waif in the Rocky Mountain silver mining camps, she had melted all her crayons into a pot that, coincidentally, also held the kind-hearted desert rats who had raised her in Colorado. Hard-hearted, cold-hearted, and a hell of a shot.

"You?" Marsha said in a tone close to admiration.

That's when Kent realized he'd been musing aloud; it's also when he realized that he had opened the last cupboard, and Caroline was growing damn heavy for such a slender woman.

"Me," Sunday said proudly.

Rex seemed nonplussed. It was obvious that the woman who had carried his child wasn't the woman he had thought she was, even before she had carried his child. Especially before, now that Kent thought about it. Amazing.

"Damn you, Montana," Maclemmon snarled, snapping them all back to the present situation.

"The hell with the woman, shoot him," Sunday said, and raised her gun.

"It could get awfully bloody," Rex said doubtfully, raising his hands as if to protect his tuxedo.

"Maybe we should just rush him," Wally suggested meekly. "Then we could shoot him. After he drops my wife, of course." He nodded. "Of course. After." But he didn't sound very hopeful, or very distressed, for that matter.

But Kent had finally found the hidden bulk of the *Bingomomicron,* and as the others abruptly found courage and strength in superior albeit wounded numbers, weaponry, and general villainy, he shoved the swooning, crooning, sighing Caroline into their midst, spun around, and sprinted out the door.

Shots were fired.

Glass was shattered.

Chips chipped from wood and plaster.

The house began to sway alarmingly, and loudly, and the ground began to vibrate.

Green light flared from the windows of the house in the basement of which was the well from which Kent had taken the *Bingomomicron;* green light began to flare in laser-like beams from the basement windows of Number 668; and green light began to lance in spear-like configurations across the dark green sky in a pattern so hypnotic that no one dared watch it for more than a few seconds without becoming dizzy and speaking in tongues.

Dogs howled.

Cats yowled.

Birds flew shrieking from their nests.

The crow fell out of the evergreen tree.

"Run!" Kent cried, matching deed to word. "Run for your lives!"

"Where?" Chita wanted to know as she ran beside him.

"I don't know," he admitted, running.

"The street," Quentin suggested, running.

"Why?" Sheila wanted to know, running but not very fast.

Quentin shrugged; he didn't know.

Kent did, however.

The only trouble was, he didn't think he had the time. The rumbling and the vibrating and trembling grew ever stronger, and it was, by his reckoning and because time flies when you're going to die, almost twelve o'clock.

✦2✦

Ivan Vlaskovich sat on the steps of someone's empty house, he couldn't remember the name except that the woman always threw rolls at him on Sundays after church, and watched the dazzling light-show in the sky. It was interesting but not fascinating. Also not fascinating but much closer was the way Number 670 had somehow caught fire, even though the family who used to live there, he couldn't remember the name, had moved out last April, just around tax time. The flames were still caught behind the windows, but he could see their shadows on the walls where there were still walls to hold the shadows. Interesting. Nothing like it back home, that was for sure, since back home a house on fire like that would have burned down hours ago, being mostly tiny and made of rotted wood and mud as they were.

He almost felt nostalgic.

He also watched the three mysterious automobiles suddenly drive away, creating a small traffic jam down by the park until the long blue car ran up on the sidewalk and around the corner. The sporty red one, his favorite color next to black, slammed into the back of the black one several times in frustration before the black one finally started its engine and drove straight through the park. That was interesting too; there were no roads in the park. He wondered what the driver was thinking of. He knew what the driver of the red car was thinking of; it chased the black car through the park and out the other side.

He waited for the crash since there wasn't a street on the other side of the park, but none came.

Now that was fascinating.

But since nothing else happened of note, he knew he'd have to be content with the burgeoning fire in Number 670, which had finally broken through the roof and was doing interesting things with the green things in the sky.

That's when he remembered the people in Number 668.

Damn, he thought in fluent Russian; all this time sitting here and watching the pretty lights and he'd completely forgotten his mission, whatever it was, he couldn't remember. He decided to sit a little longer. Maybe something would spark his memory. He grinned, he chuckled. Not bad, Ivan, not bad, he thought; making jokes in English isn't easy when you don't think the language.

He chuckled again and scratched half a flea-infested village out of his scalp.

That's when he heard the first shots.

He sat up, alarmed.

He stared, uneasy.

He looked up the street and saw chubby Amy Perkins hustling down the sidewalk, all bundled up as though it were the middle of winter.

"Good day," he said pleasantly as she passed him, even though it was the middle of the night.

She stopped, frowned in his direction, smiled when she recognized him sitting in the dark, and visibly relaxed. "Well, how are you, Ivan Vlaskovich?" she greeted in that gorgeously deep and husky voice of hers that reminded him of the steppes when they fed the cattle every spring. "And what are you doing, sitting on that porch when it's practically midnight?"

He nodded at the fire. "Waiting for the engines."

Amy turned and gasped. "My god, thank heavens you called them."

"I didn't."

"You didn't? Why not?"

"The authorities," he said, touching the side of his nose meaningfully.

She nodded. She understood. She told him she would go straight home and call the fire department herself, not mention his name, and soon everybody would be saved in the neighborhood. As she hurried on toward the park, he wondered if he should tell her about the shooting in Number 668. He didn't. She would only want to know what was going on, who was shooting who, was there any blood and was there anything she could do.

She was a nice woman.

She had a great figure for a woman whose size rivaled that of his four sisters.

But she was nosy as hell, and half the people over there would probably bleed to death before she could fix them.

More shots, and some shouting.

Now this was something he hadn't foreseen, the shouting part and those people running around the side of the house with a humongous ugly book that seemed to glow a curious shade of red. He hadn't foreseen this part at all.

Nervously he hugged his precious ironing board to his chest and considered moving to another town. But he hadn't foreseen that either, so he stayed where he was and wondered if Bog-Muggoth, the son of a bitch alien capitalistic running dog god, was going to show up like He promised. In Russia, he would have; they always showed up on time for some recreational slaughter and maiming.

The ground trembled.

Number 670 shook as the fire collapsed the roof.

Number 672 was smoldering a little too, as was Number 664.

He looked up at the sky.

He caressed the board and waited.

Three elderly gentlemen in dated but still elegant evening attire stood at the corner of Langford Place and another street, not the one by the park, and watched the flames, heard the shooting, watched the sky, heard the shouting, and considered joining the fun.

They had made it back in time after all, and it fair made them giddy.

The short one, however, slipped a pair of sunglasses over his large watery eyes and said, "I think this is not a good place to be for us tonight."

"Whyever not, Pete?" the tallest one said in a cultured but muffled accent.

"He is right, Harry," the middle-size man agreed, speaking for the first time all night. "It is not right for us to show up this late."

Harry fussed with his evening scarf as people plunged out of the dark into the middle of the street, and shots blew out half the windows of one of the houses. "Perhaps, gentlemen, you make a lot of sense."

"I mean, it just isn't done," Pete insisted. "You just don't show up and take over. It only confuses things. I just don't know what you were thinking of."

"He is right, Harry," the middle-size man agreed. "You know how Bog gets."

Harry fussed with his evening scarf.

Pete looked over the top of his sunglasses. "Lots of shooting and shouting, though."

The dogs howled.

"Ah," said the middle-size man with eyes half closed in nostalgia. "The whatever of the night, how whatever they do whatever it is they're doing."

Pete laughed, although mostly it was snorty inhaling.

Harry, on the other hand, scowled his inner distress. He was, among other things including a mad scientist and a swami, a great stickler for tradition. If you were going to quote something, then you had better quote it correctly or not quote it at all, that was his motto. His other motto was, never ever wear heavy shoes when you had to run for your life. Lug, his middle-size companion, had never understood that. Of course, Harry hardly ever understood Lug either, come to think of it; the man talked as if he had hordes of marbles in his mouth.

The cats yowled.

A frazzled crow landed at their feet, fluffed its wings, scared the hell out of the little guy, and flew off again.

"Gentlemen," Harry said, "I think I must admit that I was wrong. Perhaps we'd best leave before we're spotted, don't you agree?"

"People will die," Pete said wistfully.

"We might still warn them about the . . . book," Lug suggested tentatively as he adjusted his threadbare but still serviceable opera cape more closely around his scrawny but still serviceable neck.

Harry pointed with his silver wolf's head walking stick. "That gentleman over there, the one who looks like a baron I used to know, already has the book, Lug, as you can see. I'm afraid that if he doesn't know about it by now, we shan't be able to help him."

"People will die," said Pete with a sigh.

Suddenly a young woman with wondrous dark hair and a figure that made Pete salivate with sentiment for days past when such things mattered, raced up to them and said, "You guys know where the cops are?"

Pete cringed.

Lug was disdainful.

Harry tipped his top hat. "My dear, should you require us to fetch them, I should only be too happy to do so."

She stared at them. One by one. "Look," she said, "if you

guys aren't who you haven't said yet you are, would you mind telling me now so I can tell Kent so he won't go nuts again and forget something? Nobody on this damn street is who they were supposed to be, including me, and it's confusing, you know what I mean?"

Pete cringed.

Lug slipped back into the shadows.

Harry took several precious seconds to consider the consequences of what he might be about to do if he did it, then decided to do it, and said, "You might tell the young man with the book, my dear, that Kthulkucuth spelled backward is impossible to pronounce." He winked knowingly, tipped his hat again, and tapped his stick on the sidewalk. "But I have taken up too much of your time, I can see. Gentlemen?" he said to his companions. "Shall we go?"

He walked away.

He walked back. "And don't," he said quietly, "tell the baron who I am."

He walked away.

Chita watched him, watched them, and called, "Who?"

Wally Putney, who was the only one among the dedicated acolytes who watched television with any regularity, and even then only movies without commercials on his pirated cable system, told them that since the sacrifice had escaped, they'd have to take to the mattresses.

Caroline blushed from her supine swooned position on the dining room floor; Marsha fanned herself vigorously with her gun; and Sunday tripped over Rex's feet in her haste to race upstairs to the bedrooms.

Two minutes later she was back. "There aren't any beds," she said.

Wally shook his head and turned to John for guidance in the face of a one-track mind.

John Laste, however, was kneeling at the front parlor window, gun in hand, trying to draw a bead on Kent Montana. At the same time, Howmaster knelt beside him, rubbing his slats gingerly and desperately attempting to recall the Final Words of the Final Coming so that he wouldn't have to go out there to get the *Bingomomicron* from Montana. It wasn't working. Partly because Rex and Kenilworth were smashing the windows so they could shoot anything that moved out there in the street, and partly because the house was shaking so much that plaster rained from the ceiling onto his cowled head.

Marsha also noted that the house next door was on fire, and it would only be a matter of time before this house was ablaze as well.

"It makes no bloody difference," Maclemmon scowled. "If we don't get that damn book, we're all gonna burn."

With a groan he heaved himself to his feet, picked his way through the wreckage to the front hall, and stood at the door. Rex moved to stand beside him.

"If you go out there," the tall blond man said, "the baron will destroy the book."

"If I don't," Maclemmon snarled, "the book won't be the only thing destroyed."

Rex produced both his evilly charming smile and the Holy Vial of Blood.

Maclemmon stared at it, stared up at Rex, and matched the smile lip for lip, tooth for tooth, evil for evil. "You have a plan, I can tell."

The staircase wobbled alarmingly and some of the risers crumbled.

Rex nodded.

"Well, make it fast, m'boy," Maclemmon said with a hearty clap to Rex's shoulder.

"Make it fast."

Rex explained as the others gathered round.

The others applauded.

Maclemmon quieted them by lifting his hands, and they bowed their heads reverently as he pronounced what they hoped was an anti-blessing because they couldn't understand a damning word of it.

They scattered.

Maclemmon put his hand on the doorknob.

Sunday stayed him with a touch to his elbow. "Rex," she said, and faltered.

He stared at her.

She drew herself up. "Rex is your . . . son, isn't he?"

Something blew up; probably Number 684.

Maclemmon turned away without answering, but he didn't have to. The proud glint in his eyes told her all she needed to know, and impulsively, she kissed him on the cheek.

He smiled.

He opened the door.

He gathered his robe about him, stepped boldly onto the porch, and called Kent Montana's name.

The first of the Nine Sacred Grids, if you're counting up from the center of the Earth, melted.

It was Nine counting the other way too, but the Older Deities weren't coming from that direction.

Four distinguished and respected astronomers in Marin County, California, after standing watch for two days straight at their privately funded, government-sponsored observatory, filed fast suit with a district court judge because, they claimed hysterically, the alleged announced alleged arrival of the alleged Older Deities had destroyed their own personal religious belief systems, thus rendering them Deus disabled and unable to watch the skies without getting hives.

When, just before midnight, Eastern Standard Time, the telescope they were using was struck by a fierce bolt of vivid green lightning, setting most of the county and all of them afire, the judge threw the case out the window, picked it up from the bushes on the way home, and died in a four-car accident on his way to a holistic law meeting for the ethically challenged in newly reopened Alcatraz.

At the same time, there were tremors in Nevada, earthquakes in Madrid, tidal waves in Indonesia, vicious sandstorms in Australia, hurricanes in Ireland, typhoons in the Philippines, tornados in Germany, severe brushfires in Kenya, killer thunderstorms in Japan, flooding in the lower levels and mud slides in the mountains. Thousands died, a few more were severely injured and taken to area hospitals, and France cabled Washington to find out what the hell was going on; Washington, however, wasn't sleeping there anymore.

The second Grid melted.

Stanley Verlin turned in his adjustable hospital bed and put a quivering hand on his wife's knee. "Darling," he said, "I don't think our Sheila is coming home tonight."

Hortense Verlin buzzed her wheelchair closer to the bed and grasped her husband's quivering hand. "God, I hope so."

"It's time," said Grace Verlin from her lotus position on the floor.

And Theobald Verlin opened the door to his cage, looked out the window, and said, "Man."

Grace wrinkled her nose. "I smell smoke."

Hortense screamed and zoomed toward the door.

Stanley gasped and clutched his tank to his chest.

And Theobald suddenly realized how it must have been for his older sister all these long and torturous years, taking care of this one, taking care of that one, suffering the whining and the complaining and the whimpering and the begging, catering here and bowing and scraping there, spoon-feeding, hand-washing, ironing, vacuuming, scrubbing, painting, helping Mrs. Eddye fill potholes in her spare time, measuring medicines, controlling doses, dispensing pills . . .

He shook.

He turned.

He stared into the smoke-filled hallway, found his redemption and the coat he'd lost six months ago, and said, "Now listen up, you people, we can get out of this if we all work together. Just remember that the Verlin family love will keep us strong."

Hortense wept; Stanley choked back a sob; and Grace looked down between her folded legs and said, "Oops."

The third Grid melted.

And from the very depths of the planet Earth, and the very depths of Space, and from every corner of the globe, figuratively speaking since it's round, there came a devastating roar of such volume, of such magnitude, of such guttural rage, of such Evil, of such Horror, of such Unmitigated and Undiluted Terror, that every window in Hamtucket exploded outward, every street buckled, every door canted on its hinges, every chimney collapsed, every neon sign shorted out, every television fritzed, every lawn gnome exploded, and every human being who hadn't moved out because of the hard times and the explosion of the ice cream factory tumbled from their beds or wherever and raced to their windows where they screamed in utter fear at the fearsome sight in the sky, some of which was a reflection of the sights on Langford Place they were just as glad they couldn't see directly.

It was horrible.

This, then, was Hamtucket . . .

. . . as the world turns.

•3•

"What the hell was *that*!" Chita yelled piercingly into Kent's ear as the unearthly roaring faded into the dark green October night.

Kent shook his head, although he had a pretty good idea, and the idea, suitably embellished, suggested a time so short that there was every chance he wasn't going to make it this time, relatively speaking. He'd also be deaf if she didn't stop that yelling.

There were two large century oak trees across the street from Number 668 that hadn't fallen down yet. Quentin and Sheila were cowering behind one, Kent and Chita were ensconced behind the other. After bolting from the blatantly unhealthy protection of Number 668, they would have run then directly into the house now behind them, but it had somehow caught fire on their way there, as had most of the buildings on the block, and once the dedicated acolytes had found the range, the four of them had been pinned down behind the oaks instead.

Kent, with his back to the bark, held the *Bingomomicron;* Chita, facing him, had the guns.

"All right," he said when the night quieted again. "How does it look?"

He closed his eyes; what a stupid question. You're setting records this time.

"There are snipers," she told him.

"Hell, there're always snipers," he answered bitterly. "Every time you turn around, some jealous son of a bitch tries to get you in the back, picking at every—"

She tapped his arm and pointed.

Cautiously he looked around the tree's conveniently fat bole and saw in the upper window Marsha Furst-Laste aiming at him with her bodice revolver; he saw Rex Regal on the roof aiming at him with a collapsible rifle which wasn't collapsed anymore; he saw Wally Putney sneaking limply around the right side of the porch and dropping into the bushes with, no doubt, his gun at the ready; he saw kindly Dr. Smith in the living room window; and he saw John Smith in the triangular window by the front door, aiming something at him, he wasn't exactly sure what though he had no illusions about the purpose of the aiming.

"We're trapped," Chita noted calmly. She had, in fact, made the same depressing observation at least five or six times since returning from the corner with the cryptic message from the three elderly gentlemen. Unfortunately, the original plan had been for her to keep on going, preferably to fetch the police or the army; failing that, the organist. The three gentlemen, however, had made such a vivid impression upon her that she couldn't wait to tell him about it. Thus, the tree, the occasional pinning-down fire, and finally, Howmaster Maclemmon bellowing his name from the front porch.

"Maybe I should talk to him," Kent said.

"Maybe you could get shot."

Kent considered. "A white flag."

"We don't have one and don't look at me like that, the shirt is yellow. It matches."

So much for makeshift miracles, he thought.

Then he looked down at his hands, and a slow grin crossed his lips and kept on going to his cheeks. "Hey," he called to Quentin at the next tree, some twelve to thirteen feet away, "if you see a chance to make it clear, take it."

Quentin nodded solemnly over the clutching Sheila who once again had buried her face in his chest. He was pale, there was a trace of blood on his right shoulder where someone, most likely Marsha, had creased him, and yet the determination in his expression was inspiring in a Little Big Horn sort of way.

"Montana!" Maclemmon roared, his arrogant voice carrying over the street like thunder.

Kent took a deep breath.

Chita kissed his cheek for luck.

He kissed her cheek in thanks for the luck, kissed her lips as a deposit against withdrawals for future luck, then brought the *Bingomomicron* up in a clever use of flayed nun remnants for shield, and stepped away from the tree. Not too far away, however; he was brave, but he wanted an out if he needed it.

The fourth of the Nine Sacred Grids melted.

Still counting from the bottom.

Flames crackled.

Houses vibrated.

Windows exploded.

The ground shook.

Maclemmon moved arrogantly to the top of the steps. "I want the damn book, Montana."

Kent gave him the best baronial glare of disdain he'd ever expressed, which was enough, for the nonce, to reel the robed figure back a step and veil his face with a momentary expression of doubt and anxiety.

He recovered: "The book, or I'll destroy you all!"

"You're sounding a wee desperate," Kent said with mock sympathy. "Could it be that you're more interesting in living than I am?"

Maclemmon tripped on his robe, fell down the steps, bounded to his feet and spread his arms cheerfully. "I'm not the one who's going to die, you fool."

Kent tilted his head in feigned innocent perplexity. "Then why do you want the book?"

"Sentimental reasons."

"Ah."

Maclemmon moved to the end of the walk. "Kent."

"Howie."

A glance over his robed shoulder before Maclemmon lowered his voice to a conspiratorial level. "Kent, we're all reasonable men here, yes? We've had our differences, but all that's in the past, wouldn't you say? Give us the book, old man, and I'll make sure you survive the Final Coming Pretty Soon of the Older Deities. *And* anyone else you want to name."

"Me," Chita whispered from behind the tree.

A prolonged subterranean grumbling, a pyrotechnic pyre of sparks, the screaming of tortured wood, all signaled the collapse of a house onto its foundation.

And that's when Kent couldn't help but notice since it was

virtually right in front of him that the stately Queen Anne which harbored the well from which he had taken the humongous ugly book was absolutely untouched by any of the neighborhood's various conflagrations. Not a window broken, not a speck of paint blistered, not a clapboard scorched. Without widening his eyes, he widened his eyes.

And without moving his lips, he said sideways, "Chita, when I give the signal, I want you to pin those people down."

"All of them?"

"Just the ones with guns."

He sensed a shrug. "Okay."

"Howie," he said, louder, "I'll make you a deal."

"Hey," Chita whispered.

"What is it?" Maclemmon asked suspiciously as he moved to the curb.

Kent stepped off his curb, the ponderous book shifting slightly side to side as he saw from his extensive peripheral vision the acolytes drawing enough beads on him to make a necklace. He tried to wear a cloak of confidence, armor of unflappability, coat of calm, but he feared Maclemmon would suspect how truly afraid he was anyway. Not that it made much difference. He had, in the space of a few short seconds and in a flash of intuition, deciphered the elegant elderly gentlemen's message, and realized that he had but one chance to make the solution work.

One chance.

One life to live.

Jesus.

"Hey, psst, what's the signal?"

Maclemmon was now less than ten feet away, hands on his pudgy hips, pudgy lips curled in a sneer. "What deal, Kent?"

Kent braced himself.

Maclemmon looked at Number 668 and waved to prove to his anxious followers that he was all right. When another house collapsed, he threw his head back and laughed robustly at the dark green sky.

The cowl fell from his head.

His hair was stark white.

"Kent," he warned jovially, "don't try to con me, now. You know it's never worked before except that once, and it won't work now. You're done and delivered, old son, and I'm the one who done it."

Kent tensed.

"So. The deal?" But Maclemmon wasn't as confident as he appeared. His fingers kept snapping, his right foot kept tapping, and a faint twitch jerked at the corner of one eye.

The south end of the street buckled with a grinding roar, and both men danced to maintain their balance.

"I don't want to die," Kent said at last, jaw tight, neck muscles working.

Maclemmon smiled as a shark would smile if a shark could smile at the offer of a free lunch of Scottish caviar. "Just give me the book, and I'll put in a word."

"And the . . . the girl?" Kent said, a visible shudder racing through him.

"Of course, of course. No problem." Maclemmon's voice became steel. "The book, Montana. Give me the sacred book. Now!"

"Do you give your word of honor?"

Maclemmon smirked. "As a gentleman," and he bowed.

Another house collapsed, and Sheila screamed.

Kent looked, he couldn't help it, it was automatic and she was so damn loud, and saw the saintly girl racing headlong up the street toward her flame-engulfed home, Quentin racing along behind her.

There were no shots.

Soon they vanished into the thickening smoke, and the sudden thickening fog that had moved in on them while the houses were burning, unless, of course, it was only more smoke from other burning houses in other parts of town. It was difficult to tell; everything stank of burning houses.

But at least, he thought, the kids have escaped.

For the time being.

"Something else," he said, turning back to the pudgy cowled figure who had so obviously faked his own death it was almost criminal to bring it up. "Something else."

Maclemmon snorted impatiently. "What?"

"Your hair. What happened to your hair?"

Maclemmon grew pale and scrambled the cowl back over his head. "Never you mind."

"Something frightened you."

Maclemmon started, recovered, swallowed, sneered. "Not me, Kent. You know me."

Kent wondered if indeed he knew Howie at all anymore. "Then there's something else. I'd hoped you'd tell me—"

"Enough!" Maclemmon spat, and raised his right hand high over his head. "This hand," he declared solemnly, looking up at his right hand, "is going to come down in about five seconds. When it does, all those people back there, and up there, and over there, are going to shoot you. And I will have the book. And you will be dead. Your choice, Kent. So choose."

"What about the something else?"

"I don't give a tinker's damn about the something else. You're trying to bilk me again, Kent, you stubborn devil, and it won't happen."

Kent looked at his watch.

Maclemmon looked at his watch.

Chita whispered, "The signal, what's the damn signal?"

Suddenly across the sky and from out of the house next to the one Kent had inherited and was supposed to have stayed in but didn't, green light flared and flashed and swept and crisscrossed and circled and blossomed and bloomed; the trees swayed as if buffeted by a powerful, otherworldly wind; cracks appeared in the tarmac and concrete; sirens cried in the distance; and thick clouds of dark green and darker black began to gather over the small town of Hamtucket, Rhode Island.

"Two seconds," Maclemmon announced generously.

Kent wished his life would flash across his eyes so he could make a few minor adjustments.

"One second."

That awful roaring began again, this time much quieter, and much, much closer.

"Wait," said Kent calmly as Maclemmon's hand came down.

"What?" The hand paused halfway.

Kent held out the book. "The book."

Maclemmon looked at him sideways, one eye closed, the other not sure. "What's the catch?"

"None."

"You sure?"

"Absolutely."

"No bilking?"

Kent laughed. "Me? Bilk the expert?"

Maclemmon laughed with him. "You? Bilk the expert?"

"Take the book, man, and be done with it. You've given your word, and I accept that."

Maclemmon crossed the space between them in a single whooping bound. "Then you," he said cackling, "are a bleedin' idiot."

The fifth of the Nine Sacred Grids melted.

Maclemmon reached for the book.

Kent pulled it away.

Maclemmon scowled, slightly off-balance before he'd been reaching for the book. As a result, Kent was able to spin him neatly around with his free hand and whisper, "Your slip's showing, Howie."

At the same time, the dedicated acolytes, seeing the vital right hand come down, opened fire.

"Is that the signal?" Chita whispered.

And Kent ducked as best he could behind the pudgy robed figure, and counted to ten while at least three times that many bullets perforated the robe, the cowl, the sandals, the T-shirt underneath, the rainbow boxer shorts, and eight of the most vital nonmusical organs in Maclemmon's prancing, spinning, dancing, jerking body.

"That's the signal," Chita decided.

She opened fire.

At the same time, though not quite the same time as the other time, Kent lunged to his feet and sprinted in an awkward crouch across the road, holding the book up in case the acolytes tried to stop him, a rather unlikely event since they were pinned down by Chita's ferocious barrage.

At least most of them were pinned down.

John Laste wasn't pinned down; he was dead with a bullet to his wallet which he kept in his evening jacket just in case. Nor was Sunday pinned down, except by Kenilworth Smith, who had decided that shooting barons wasn't medically correct and wanted to spend his last moments in biological research, the genetic stuff having gone nowhere. Nor, in fact, were Wally and Marsha pinned down since, on the one hand, bushes offered no protection at all from bullets and, on the other hand, neither did glass windows.

Caroline was still swooned on the dining room floor.

But somebody was still shooting at him as he vaulted the picket fence in front of the Queen Anne, zig-zagged across the yard, and sprang onto the porch; and that somebody was doing a damn good job of almost hitting him, too. He was forced to press himself against, and preferably into, the locked front door as bullets whizzed and winged and pinged and creased around him in such mindless fury that he feared he'd never be able to complete the second part of the plan he had thought of while bargaining with Maclemmon.

Then Chita stopped shooting.

He looked as best he dared across the street and saw, with horror, the signal she sent him that told him, in rather obscene Latin gestures, that she was out of ammunition.

The somebody wasn't, however; he directed his fire at Chita, who yelped and ducked back behind the tree.

Kent, who was getting used to not wasting time, wasted no time charging madly across the porch and leaping off the other end, a drastic response required of him upon remembering that the basement door was bolted, banded, and covered with mystic signs. He raced along the side of the house, discovered an outside basement door, flung it open, ran down the steps, and skidded to a halt.

The sixth Sacred Grid melted.

The basement was as neat as he remembered it, but it was awfully green. Curiously enough, the devastation and disturbances affecting the outside world were muted in here, except for the snarling and slavering and growling and roaring that rose from the well in the middle of the floor.

Kent had no desire to see what was down there. Yet, if he was right, if he had interpreted the mysterious message correctly, he would have to see what was down there, because what was down there was coming up here, and it had to get up here before he could do what he had to do to make sure that it wouldn't get out of here.

If he was wrong, on the other hand, he was cooked.

If he was wrong, he would see what no other human being has seen in thousands of years; he would see the terrible visage of Bog-Muggoth, and his other ugly god buddies; he would see, and he would go permanently . . . totally . . . mad.

Dead, then, or nuts.
Him, then, or the world.
Dead, then, or nuts.

The seventh Sacred Grid melted.

Kent heard the bubbling and hissing as the grid's steel bars melted; he heard the scrabbling and scraping of long sharp claws digging into the well's walls; he heard heavy rasping bubbling hissing breathing as the owner of those claws clawed its way up the well's walls.

He heard footsteps in the tunnel.

Amazing.

He hurried to the well, did not look down, but rested the *Bingomomicron* on the lip.

Rex Regal, as untidy as he'd ever been in his life, burst into the room and aimed his uncollapsed collapsible rifle at Kent's heart.

"The book," said Rex.

Kent smiled. "No."

Rex paled. "What do you mean, no?"

Kent opened the *Bingomomicron* to a random page, frowned at the unintelligible language inscribed there, raised an eyebrow at the graphic woodcut impression on the facing page, and turned the page. More words he couldn't read, and more pictures and illustrations that, in a man with a weaker constitution, would have produced severe abdominal contractions.

"What are you doing?" Rex demanded.

"Browsing," Kent answered calmly.

"I'll kill you. Give me the book."

"You can kill me," Kent said, "but the book isn't going to do you a damn bit of good."

Rex took a step closer. "What are you talking about? We must have the Final Words of the Final Coming or we'll all be murdered in our beds!"

Kent nodded toward the bubbling hissing clawing heavy breathing thing making its way toward the eighth Sacred Grid. "I don't think Bog-Muggoth needs landing directions now."

Rex gaped. "My god." In his extreme distress, he raked his fingers through his hair. "You were right all along. We've been tricked." He glanced at the ceiling. "They're not coming from outer space after all."

"Oh yes they are," Kent corrected.

Rex looked at the well.

The basement door wrenched open and Chita ran down the steps, a gun in each hand.

She stared at Kent, she stared at Rex, she stared at the well. "Do I have timing or what?"

"How did you get here?" Kent asked.

"Through the door."

"Are you all right?"

"The book!" Rex screamed.

She shrugged her unwounded shoulder. "I'll live."

"Like hell, you woman you," Rex snarled, whirled, and aimed the rifle at her breast, changed his mind and aimed it at her face, changed his mind and aimed it at her left kneecap.

Chita shot him.

Rex staggered backward and collided with the wall.

Kent closed the *Bingomomicron* and peered over the lip of the well.

The eighth Sacred Grid melted.

Green; nothing but swirling clouds of green in every hue and every shade. Yet, beneath that swirling putrescent green was a dark putrescent figure that Kent realized immediately was but the anthropomorphic visualization of an Older Deity whose true image would be known only when it broke through the final Sacred Grid.

He waited.

He had to wait.

If he moved too soon, it would be too soon and all would be lost; if he moved too late, all would be lost.

His timing had to be perfect.

Rex fired at Chita.

Hissing.

Bubbling.

Clawing.

Chita shot Rex, who fell back against the wall again.

Kent glanced at his watch, and wondered with a brief surge of inopportune curiosity just what it was that had driven Howmaster Maclemmon to tempt such an indescribable fate, all for the dubious honor of becoming ruler of a world that would have been nothing but desolation as far as the alien eye could see; what voracious needs within him, what childhood abuses and adult mistreatment and lifelong deprivations had been his that he had been blinded to the fool that he really was, to the pathetic pudgy idiot he had turned out to be; what hell had he gone through to make him turn out this way?

Kent didn't know; he figured Howie was just a prick.

Rex shot at Chita.

Bubbling.

Clawing.

Hissing.

Scratching.

Chita shot Rex, ruined his tuxedo, and Rex fell back against the basement wall again.

The room began to shake, the well began to crumble, and the green intensified to an almost blinding green with some gold around the edges.

Rex began to sag. "The book," he gasped as he tried to keep his lapels in line. "Please. Use . . . the . . . book."

Kent shook his head. "I told you—it won't do any good."

Blood bubbled ever so faintly at a corner of his mouth. His lips worked. His jaw worked. His eyes began to close. "Why?" he whispered.

"Because," Kent said.

The well's walls began to fall into the well.

"Oh Lord," Rex called to his former employer, for such was Kent in the old days when he had hired Rex the handsome footman for the express purpose of distracting his nanny from her mother-inspired duties; but the plan had failed because Rex, for a while, fell madly in love with Nanny and became her ally in attempted baroncide. "Lord, sir, I don't want to live in a world dominated by those . . . creatures. I would rather die."

Chita shot him.

And Kent, using an upraised arm to protect him from the rays of the intensified green exploding from the well, leaned over, and saw the putrescent creature curl its slimy claws around the bars of the ninth of the Nine Sacred Grids.

He saw its eyes; they were green.

He saw its writhing hair; it was green.

He saw things no man or baron was ever meant to see.

He saw the bars begin to twist and melt.

"Kent!" Chita cried.

And Kent Montana took the *Bingomomicron* in his hands, raised it over his head . . .

. . . and threw it down the well.

He ran for the stairs.

Chita ran for the door.

Bog-Muggoth The Older Deity set the melting steel bars of the Ninth Sacred Grid aflame, just as the *Bingomomicron* impaled itself on one of his claws.

Kent sprinted for the front door, passing Chita somewhere in the dining room.

Bog-Muggoth saw what it had done.

Kent opened the front door.

Bog-Muggoth opened its myriad green eyes in a spacial god expression of shock.

Kent grabbed Chita's hand and they ran for the street.

But Bog-Muggoth, for all his power and disgusting magnificence, could not prevent the *Bingomomicron* from bursting into crimson and scarlet flame, could not prevent the spells he himself had created from taking effect, could not prevent the spirals of time and space from tightening around every one of his scaled and hairy necks, could not prevent those spirals from loosening his grip on the well's wall, could not prevent himself from being dragged helplessly by those spirals back down, then out, then into the Void of the Space Place where the other Older Deities waited.

For him.

Or it.

Breathlessly Kent reached the other side of the street, but he could not find anyplace to hide. Everything was in flames; everything was destroyed; everything was gone.

He turned and held Chita to his side, and together they faced Number 666, Langford Place, watching with horror and pride and terror and satisfaction and indescribable something else as the stately Queen Anne didn't so much blow up as implode in an explosion that was, because of the implosion, absolutely and terrifyingly silent. Crimson fire. Scarlet flame. Red smoke. Green hair. Unmercifully sucked into a whirling spiral of space that had no dimension and all dimensions, that had no time and was of all Time, that had no sound and was pretty quiet.

And then, for just a moment, everything froze.

"Oh," said Chita.

"Damn," said Kent Montana.

A tentacle, blue as a pure spring sky after a gentle morning shower, shot out of the space-spiral cloud and grabbed the bodies of Howmaster Maclemmon and Wally Putney; then it punched through the walls of Number 668, and plucked out the bodies, not all of them dead yet, of Marsha Furst-Laste and John Laste, of Sunday Eddye and kindly Dr. Kenilworth Smith, and lastly of Caroline Putney, still in her swoon.

It dragged them into the Void.

Not one of them screamed, although Caroline moaned a little.

Then the space-spiral flared, faded, flared, spun, and abruptly winked out with a clap of thunder that blew Kent and Chita to the ground.

And nothing was left but the sound of gentle weeping.

– IX –

The Last Episode

✦1✦

They sat on two tiny chairs did Kent Montana and Chita Juarel, two tiny chairs with robins and chickadees stenciled on the seats. And the chairs were on the porch of Number 668.

It was mid-morning. Saturday. The sky and the air were autumn crisp and clean, there was the scent of burning leaves on a soft autumn breeze, and children had come out to play in their yards, and in the park where a headless winged marble woman dribbled water into a cracked marble bowl.

"It was a dream thing, right?" Chita said, looking around the neighborhood. "If it was one of those dream things, I'm really going to be annoyed. Really."

Kent only smiled.

To the casual observer, and to the people who lived here as well, there was absolutely nothing wrong with Langford Place. Oh, the houses were still a little faded, the street not quite perfectly paved, the sidewalks still a little cracked, and the lawns still spiked with stubborn fall weeds; but otherwise, there was no sign of fire or brimstone or destruction or calamity. Except for the vacant lot with the big hole in it to his left.

He stretched. He groaned pleasantly. He looked to his right and saw Ivan Vlaskovich racing full speed up the middle of the street, ironing board in hand, its bottom gleaming as if waxed. When the Russian peasant tripped, fell on the board, and sailed whooping and laughing toward the intersection, Kent turned to Chita and said with a perfectly straight face, "Serf's up."

She hit him.

He didn't care; he'd been waiting all night to say that, and he didn't care a bit. It hurt, though; she packed a wallop that feisty woman did.

"So what happened?" she wanted to know.

"We saved the world."

"Well, hell, I know that, but how?"

"You shot Rex, and I burned the book."

"Right." She twisted around on her chair. "So how come you didn't throw the book into one of the burning houses?"

"Because," he said blandly, "they weren't burning."

"I can see that," she snapped, "but they were burning, you know?"

Amy Perkins hustled by on her way to work. She waved, winked at Chita, frowned when she realized Chita wasn't Hester but looked awfully familiar, and almost came up the walk to find out what had happened. Kent stared at her. Her smile weakened, and she went on. Barons were pretty good at that sort of thing when they had to be.

"Like everything else," he said, breathing in the beautiful air, "it was an illusion. I knew it when I saw Ivan sitting on some steps and not getting fried. That's when I knew that the book had to be burned in real fire, the kind of fire that only the Older Deities could generate. So . . ."

She nodded. "Nice work."

Quentin and Sheila stepped arm-in-arm out of their undamaged house, waved enthusiastically to Kent and Chita, and stepped aside to allow Sheila's mother to zoom out and down the steps, then her father in his bed specially adapted for local traffic by Quentin, then her brother who was on a cellular telephone talking to his broker, and finally, carrying a little bundle of newly minted joy, her sister.

They stood in a line and waved in the sunlight.

"Jesus," said Chita.

Kent waved royally back. "Be kind," he said without moving his lips. "Quentin is an orphan now, remember? It's going to take some doing to get used to that family."

Hortense and Ivan began a race toward the park; Stanley tried to join them but his bed got stuck in third.

Laughter floated over the street.

Suddenly Chita snapped her fingers.

He frowned.

"The message," she said. "That weird guy, Harry?, with the message. What the hell did it mean?"

"Ah." He loved being smug; it really pissed her off. "It meant that since it's impossible to say Kthulkucuth backward, and damn difficult frontward, then it was also impossible to say anything in the *Bingomomicron* that would affect the Older Whatevers, no matter what Howie thought, since the crucial Final Words were, in fact, backward." He shook his head. "They bilked him, the poor sod. Boy, did they bilk him."

She stared.

He shrugged.

She said, "Htucukluhtk," and only spit a little.

Shit, Kent thought.

A minute passed for all the implications, horrors, and feelings of complete but familiar stupidity to sink in.

Then Chita sniffed, reached behind her chair and pulled her suitcase around. "So. What now?"

"Now," he said, clasping his hands behind his head, "I wait for the attorney to come by, see that I'm here, see that I'm here and alive and not nuts, so he can hand me the final papers. And then . . ." He shrugged.

The organ played a happy tune.

"You still have a gun?" he asked.

"You know," she answered, adroitly ignoring the testy request, "you didn't stay in the house *all* night."

He nodded.

"In fact, we kind of camped out on the lawn over there after the house went smackers."

He nodded, and lowered his arms.

"Point is, you kind of didn't do what you were supposed to do, you know?"

Catches, he thought; Jesus Christ, even after saving the world, there're still goddamn catches.

He looked at her.

She grinned, and poked her suitcase with one foot. "I'm going to Arizona this afternoon. Got a job cutting down banana trees on a plantation."

"Chita. Chita, there are no banana tree plantations in Arizona."

"I know that. You know that. So when I get there, and I sue the ass off the guy that gave me the job, I'm gonna have some extra cash to invest, you know what I mean?"

Catches.

He checked his hair.

The sound of a small engine drifting down the street.

"So," she continued, cleaning her nails with the butcher knife, "that guy that always comes here around this time?"

"Him," Kent said, pointing to a man in a denim jacket, western boots, and a worn but lovable grey western hat riding down the sidewalk on a spiffy red motor scooter.

"Yep. He works for you now, right? Bringing new scripts and stuff?"

Slowly. Very slowly: "Yes."

The man stopped, reached into his saddlebag, pulled out a large package, and handed it to Kent over the railing. He still had his beard, but it was a little greyer these days. "Close call, huh?"

"You said it," Chita answered before Kent could open his mouth. She nodded toward the package. "Give me a hint. He going to Rio next? Paris? London? Moscow? Berlin? Tokyo? Honolulu?"

The messenger grinned as he got back on the spiffy red scooter. "Nope."

"Oh . . . Jesus," Kent whispered when he tore the package open and peeked at the first page.

"Where?" Chita asked eagerly. "I invest in your pictures, I want to see these places too, get the company to pay for it."

The scooter zoomed away, beating the bed by a length and Hortense by two.

"Fine," Kent said, and handed it over. He stood, stretched, laughed at his new-found, suddenly heady and exciting artistic freedom, and kissed Chita soundly on the top of her head before going inside to fetch his own suitcase, which was still up in the room that would have been his bedroom if it had had a bed.

He heard Chita scream when he was halfway up the stairs.

He heard the front door slam open when he reached the top landing.

"Yo, Lord!" she yelled.

He looked down.

She held up the package as if she was going to throw it. "You're kidding, right?"

He laughed and blew her a kiss.

"Goddamnit, Montana!"

He walked away, still laughing.

"Albuquerque? We're going to goddamn Albuquerque?"

And the organ, electronically enhanced to sound like a full, lush, romantically triumphant orchestra, played on.

✦2✦

"ALBUQUERQUE?"

– X –

The Credits, and One Commercial

THE CREDITS

STARRING AS THEMSELVES:

Bog-Muggoth
Quentin Eddye
Pilandra Eddye
Chita Juarel
Boris Karloff
Kthulkucuth
Marsha Laste
John Laste
Peter Lorre
Bela Lugosi
Howmaster Maclemmon
Kent Montana
Amy Perkins
Wally Putney
Caroline Putney
Rex Regal
Kenilworth Smith
Grace Verlin
Theobald Verlin
Hortense Verlin
Stanley Verlin
Sheila Verlin
Ivan Vlaskovich

WITH SPECIAL APPEARANCES BY:

The Elegant Old Man................................ Boris Karloff
The Mumble-Mouth Old Man .... Bela Lugosi
The Short Old Man .... Peter Lorre
Messenger .... Mysterious Person

And:

STANLEY, THE DAREDEVIL CROW

Producer .... Northgate 386/20
Director .... Lionel Fenn
Writer .... Lionel Fenn
Editor .... Ginjer Buchanan
Titles .... Edward Bryant
Additional Dialogue .... Harlan Ellison
Drivers .... Arnold Palmer
Locations .... Over There
Interpreter .... Irwin Corey

Monster Role Models .... Godzilla, Mothra, Mussolini
Well .... Jack Benny
Miss Juarel's Ruffles .... Ridges of Hamtucket
Mr. Montana's Hair .... Bugs Bunny
Organ .... (too easy)
Gutted Oyster .... Disgusting

AND SPECIAL THANKS TO:

Mr. Harlan Ellison, for remembering our gal (well, not *our* gal) from Colorado; the Kent Montana Fan Club for clips from *Passions and Power;* and the Hamtucket, Rhode Island, Bold and Beautiful Garden League and Literary Society, Santa Barbara Division, for the expertise required to re-create the convolutions, inconsistencies, and genealogy charts so vital to all continuing daytime dramas. They also gave us pictures, but we didn't use them.

THE COMMERCIAL

This is a thoroughly immodest, but tastefully low-key, pitch for **HAGGIS,** the official newsletter of the Kent Montana Fan Club, a totally new, cheap but kind of classy publication designed to enhance, complement, and unashamedly shill the Kent Montana/Lionel Fenn filmatic book experience. There are no pretensions here. There are no intellectual assaults upon your vital critical thinking abilities. **HAGGIS** is designed for no other reason than to have some ridiculous fun, tell some truly awful jokes, write really long sentences, and generally mess around with reality a little, a commodity we have, in our opinion, too damn much of these days.

If you're squeamish, $3.00 (U.S.) will get you the latest issue by return mail; if you're bold, daring, and adventurous, $12.00 (U.S.) will get you five sort of packed issues (one year). Checks in either amount payable to Kent Montana Fan Club (or C. Grant) at the editorial/subscription address of:

PO Box 97, Newton, NJ 07860

No kidding.

No guarantees either, but what the hell.